The

Dreams

Between

Us

Brooke Riley

For anyone who has ever felt alone. For the dreamers searching for an escape. For the ones who feel lost and dream of being found. This is for you.

PROLOGUE

Rook

BEFORE THE DARKNESS seeped into my veins and fractured my heart, there was light. But now, all that I touch, all that I feel in the space between skin and bones, is power. Raw, unbridled power.

The kind of power that society fears. Uncontrollable. Wild.

Power that society leaders wish they could wield and use for their own gain. They think they have power. But it's pitiful and weak compared to my own, to the absolute species I have been made into. Power is nothing without a master who knows how to control it.

Only the Shadow Council and the Society of Shadows know how to wield it.

I have the life force of shadows swirling inside of me, wishing to be unleashed.

A hunger exists inside me to feast on the souls I'm asked to collect. The power that flows through me is unmatched. I've tasted the sting of it on my tongue, the soothing, sweet honey of its truest form.

Addictive.

Intoxicating.

Yet, despite the craving that has manifested inside me, I find the desire to consume human souls repulsive. Watching their life force drain from their body as they fade into oblivion, ceasing to exist. There is a part of me that still holds onto my human form and remembers who I am, and how I became this... creature.

A broken heart, a broken family, a broken life. So many things break in life, and for me, it became unbearable. I wanted to stop my suffering. But before stepping from the ledge, ending the human I used to be, something wrapped its icy tendrils around me. It prevented me from taking the fall.

You could heal, it whispered in my ear.

I didn't want death. I wanted to escape. The Shadow Council heard my soul crying for something more than this dreadful human existence.

A shadow appeared near me, whispering promises of something unheard of.

I struck a deal with the shadowy figure that saved me. I became like him. I became an essence of shadow, and so began my hunger.

An Umbra is what they called me—now governed by the Council of Shadows. A ruling government in the Shadow Realm. A place of dreams and nightmares. They gave me the power to live without my heart shattered. To never have to feel any of the hard human emotions breaking me down. In return, I fulfill a quota, draining souls of their life force. The power of nightmares and fear is what keeps the Shadow Realm alive. I traded one prison for another.

But now, there is power coursing through my veins, giving me strength.

And I am addicted to how it feels.

However, as I stand in front of the Shadow Council now, fear grips at the human traces of my heart. The spotlight burns me slowly, keeping me still. Their long semi-circular table curves around me. Everything is shrouded in shadow and darkness. I cannot see one other being, one other Umbra. No faces. No eyes. Only their whispers tell me they are here in this room with me.

I've not felt human emotion since becoming an Umbra. But I'm not so out of touch with what's left of my humanity that I've forgotten what fear feels like.

"Rook." One of the Umbra speaks in an icy voice. "You have been given a quota to fill. Yet you return empty-handed. What do you say for yourself?"

"I have not come across any soul that speaks to me."

The Council hisses and whispers to each other, then another member says, "To stay among us, the Umbra, you are to consume four souls before the start of winter solstice."

"Where will I find four souls?"

"Go amongst the humans; be in their realms. You've avoided the human realm more than any Umbra has this season. If you wish to live, you *will* consume four souls. Now be gone, and do not return until your quota is complete."

I'm cast into darkness; the spotlight that was burning bright on me is switched off. It's not going to be easy, finding four souls in the human world that I can manipulate.

But as I fly through the realm, an idea strikes me.

Maybe it won't be so hard to find souls if I already know of some that deserve to be trapped in their nightmares and consumed.

My past is a web of pain and misery. It couldn't hurt to use those who burned me, who inflicted such pain upon me—who are the very reason that I joined the shadows.

A wicked smile inches its way up my face.

It's time for revenge.

1

Ophelia

DARK POP MUSIC streams from the speakers mounted to the corners of the walls. I close my eyes, inhaling the smell of books and coffee, letting the music seep into my bones and soothe me. Any lingering stress melts away, fading into the background. I drum my fingers to the beat as I organize the books on the shelf closest to the counter. For a moment, everything is perfect.

The swish of a curtain that divides the front of the store from the back room signals Priya's arrival. "Ophelia...did you take over my speakers with your playlist again?"

My eyes open to see my boss standing behind the counter. Her brown hands rest on her narrow hips in mock anger, her dark brows arched in a question. But behind the attempt to look stern, there's a light in her chocolate brown eyes. Amusement that matches the smile tugging on her lips. It falls apart as she shakes her head, unable to keep up the act any longer. She brushes her shoulder-length dark hair out of her face, still smiling.

"Maybe I did." I smirk. "Or perhaps the radio station is finally gaining taste."

"So the classical music station decided to start playing your punk music?"

I rise from my seat on the floor where I have been organizing a stack of books on a lower shelf. "First of all, this isn't punk. There's no screaming or whining about your parents in these songs. This is quality music. Second, I needed something edgier than Bach and Brahms."

It's Priya's turn to smirk now. I know she doesn't care too much about what plays on her speakers. But she loves to tease me.

"As long as you put it back to the store's playlist once you're finished with your work. music."

"You know, my music fits the vibe of the store way more."

Priya shakes her head, never losing her smile. She begins organizing some books and figurines behind the counter.

Darkest Night Bookstore is a shadowy, atmospheric place. Dark tapestries, navy blue and black, hang from the walls. The bookshelves are black, with fake ivy on some of them. Fairy lights hang from the ceiling, giving the room a warm glow. Two windows at the front of the store bring in a lot of natural light. The recessed lighting in the ceiling gives the same warm glow as the fairy lights.

This place was my safe haven growing up. Priya

was in her mid-twenties when she opened it with her husband ten years ago. Before he became her *estranged* husband.

They were still running the place together when I was thirteen. I remember saving up the money to come in here and buy a book every few weeks. Of course, I wasn't alone in my book-buying endeavors. But that was a different time.

One I don't care to reflect on.

I start to move towards the back bookshelves, noticing that some books aren't where they belong. As I organize, the bell above the door rings and I hear Priya greet the customer. We're slow for a Wednesday. This place is somewhat of a tourist attraction to our sleepy little town, but today there aren't many customers.

"Do you need help finding something?" Priya asks the customer, but her voice is tight, almost strained.

I reshelve some books that were left on the floor.

"No, I'm just... looking around," the customer says.

I freeze. I glance around the corner, but from where I am, I can't see the door. Something tugs at my heart, begging me to go to the front and see who this is. My mind must be playing games with me. Because there is no possibility that it's who I think it is.

But that voice...

My mind fills with a flash of blue eyes and dark hair, the smell of old leather journals and books. Summers lying in the grass, under the old oak tree in the park, reading through a shared book together. It couldn't be, though. *He* only comes to town every few months, and *he* surely wouldn't set foot in this store.

Not after all this time.

I'm frozen where I am as the sound of footfalls nears, then retreats. Almost imperceptible. Almost as if they don't exist.

I set down the book in my hand, unable to take the uncertainty any longer. I make my way through the rows of shelves, but the bell rings again before I make my way to the front. And when I finally emerge to the light, Priya is alone. Her smile is calm and her eyes are relaxed.

She'd tell me if it was *him*.

Wouldn't she?

"Finished with the back corner?" she asks, flipping through one of the few magazines she orders for the store each month.

"Almost. I have a few more books to fix."

"Okay. When you're done, let me know. I think I'm closing early. It's been pretty slow today."

"Yeah," I say softly, heading back to my corner. I'm not one to think of the past unless it comes back up. But I'd know that deep voice anywhere, even though it's gotten deeper since I've heard it. He only said one thing.

One sentence.

Yet it repeats in my mind like it was something more.

I hate how I'd know him anywhere. I hate that not even the passage of time can make the memories fade away into oblivion.

I will always know Atlas Jameson, in the depths of my soul, whether I want to or not.

At least he's gone now. Priya never hinted to him

that I was here. She probably wanted to protect me from any more hurt caused by his actions.

But she can't protect me from what's already happened.

I finish with the books not long after. I pull my coat on and grab my purse from the break room. "I'll see you tomorrow," I say to Priya.

"Enjoy the rest of your day," she says with a kind smile, following me to the door. I glance back once more. Priya waves before locking the door behind me, but there's a hint of worry in her eyes as she watches me go. Worry that I will find something outside the shop that I don't want to find.

There's an ache in my chest, something tugging me back to memories I don't want to visit. I don't want to think about the past. Not when I've come so far in healing my heart.

The autumn wind brushes against my face, blowing my hair around. Leaves tangle and turn through the air. Something about the smell of it all is breathtaking.

Or maybe I romanticize too much.

I glance over at Every Brew Café, to a boy with dark hair and soft eyes sitting at a table in the outside space. His lightweight hoodie looks too thin for the season. But I know he's not cold; he's always one to feel warm even in the coldest of winters.

I blink, thinking I must be going crazy. My heart picks up its pace as I hurry past, not wanting him to see me.

I'm losing my mind. That's all. There's no way. *Just keep walking.*

Something inside me yearns to look back, but I refuse. It's not him. It can't be him.

My mind wanders through memories I've long since buried as I finish my walk home. I hate the way I'm thinking of everything once again.

I enter my lonely house, empty and quiet. My dad is working either his second or third shift, and won't be home until tomorrow afternoon.

Sometimes the quiet is loud. I have to steady my breath to prevent the tears building up behind my eyes from falling. I'm not going to cry over Atlas Jameson after all these years.

I shrug off my coat, hanging it on the rack with my purse.

Tears still sting in my eyes, causing me to blink rapidly. I refuse to let them fall.

Erasing a whole year from your mind is hard. But I've done it before. I can't afford to let all my work go to waste.

I shudder at the sudden chill in the room. "What am I supposed to do?" I say out loud. No one's listening. But sometimes I talk out loud, hoping for some sort of answer.

But that's not how anything works.

As the evening light wanes, I find myself in the kitchen. The only sound in the apartment is the stir-fry sizzling in the skillet. I usually play music while I cook, but even that won't take the edge off now.

The aroma of peppers and onions fills the house, but I barely notice it; my mind is running rampant elsewhere. Even the taste of the food is dull to my senses, despite the fresh seasonings.

Nothing is going to cure the terrible taste Atlas leaves in my mouth.

I finish eating my dinner, and then find myself in my room. I wash my face and change into my pajamas before collapsing onto my bed. Staring up at the ceiling, I will myself to forget. To let it all go. It doesn't matter if he's in town visiting his mom. It doesn't matter that he decided to set foot in the one place I'm safe.

It's been five years. I've lived long enough without him to not be affected anymore.

But it's a lie. The emotions are too heavy, too broken for me to fight through.

Everything in my being desires to be wrong. But I know that I will never forget the voice or the face of the one person who promised to always be there.

It's us against the world.

The words repeat like a broken record, stuck on one line of a song, echoing in my ears.

He said it like a promise he intended to keep. But promises were broken, and he skipped town before I could catch my breath.

I will not break for him again.

2
Ophelia

Thirteen Years Old

I READ THE final words in the book, and then hand it over to Atlas. He smirks as he lies in the grass on his stomach, parallel to my outstretched legs. His eyes breeze through the words; he's always been a faster reader than I am. I wait patiently, wanting to see how he feels about the ending. I pull blades of grass from the ground, tying them together into a small wreath. Atlas murmurs to himself, catching my attention again.

I watch his face for any emotion. I wait for his brow to furrow, his eyes to widen at the plot twist. Or maybe he'll even throw the book across the grass in frustration like I was tempted to do.

Will he be as happy as I am with that ending?

Or will he hate it?

We don't often agree on books. By the time we

finish discussing one, we're usually ready to move on to the next.

He shuts it with a loud thump, letting it fall to the grass next to him. As I expected, his brow is furrowed, and his eyes are burning with a frustration I only ever see him get when a book has annoyed him.

He hates it.

"All of that build-up just for him to die?"

I smirk. "That's the point. He fought—in vain—to become everything he wasn't. And in the pursuit of something impure, he lost himself. It's symbolic."

Atlas rolls his eyes as he turns onto his stomach, then rises to his feet. "It's depressing. Don't you ever want to see the characters succeed in the end?"

I shrug. "Sure. But seeing them fail is more realistic."

Atlas offers his hand, helping me to my feet. He runs his free hand through his hair, contemplating. "Succeeding isn't unrealistic. I'm going to pick the book next time."

I laugh. "I didn't know it was going to have a sad ending. I picked it for the cover."

Atlas shakes his head, grinning. "I guess I'd better offer to mow the yard again so I can get some money."

The same tradition. The same chores. The same five-dollar bills saved up to buy one book from the store. All of it feels right. Natural. It's what we've done for a while now, and probably something we'll continue to do until we're old enough to have jobs to pay for the books.

Atlas glances at his phone, checking the time. "We should head home. My parents will be looking for us."

He says *us* because that's the other routine. My dad won't be wondering where I am and what I'm doing because he isn't home. He's always working, trying to balance raising me with two jobs; he's hardly ever home these days except for a brief moment after dinner time. He'll show up before I'm going to bed, sleep through the night, then he'll be off to work before I'm finished eating breakfast.

He worries, despite my reassurances. He knows full well I'm spending my free time with Atlas and his family. Besides that, we have a system. Every two hours, I text my dad, letting him know I'm alive. Letting him know where I am.

None of this is by his choice, but it's easier when I'm at school and he doesn't have to worry about me being alone. Summer is different. But school will start again soon. And then he won't have to worry.

Atlas walks beside me through town, holding the book closely.

"I wish it would stay like this forever," I say.

"Like what?"

"Simple. Us reading in the park. Going to your house for dinner. Sitting in your backyard after dark and naming constellations in the sky."

He smiles. "It's always going to be that way. It's us against the world, remember?"

A quote he picked up from a book we read a few months ago had quickly become our motto. The book was about two best friends on a journey to save their kingdom.

Our lives aren't so dramatic, but when the world feels like it's caving in, he always comforts me with that quote.

Our promise.

Our vow.

I stop walking and he stops, too. I hold my pinky finger out towards him. "Promise me."

He hooks his finger with mine. "I promise we will always be this way. Even when we're old and have gray hair. We'll always be best friends."

I laugh. The idea of being old is so far away.

We make it to his house and everything is as it should be. Dinner with his family. Constellations in his backyard. His dad trailing behind as Atlas walks me back home. When we get there, Atlas walks me to the porch, as he always does, then he and his dad wait until I'm inside to leave.

I lock the door. The house is dark, so I turn on a lamp in the living room for my dad. He'll be here soon, but I don't want him stumbling around looking for a light switch.

It's no fun being here by myself. I know Atlas hates leaving me alone, too. But I don't have much of a choice. My dad is constantly working to provide for me. And my mom left us when I was only two, not wanting to be a wife or a mother anymore.

There are no pictures of her lining the hallways. Just me and my dad. Sometimes me with cousins or other family.

I do have one picture of my mom. I take after her, as much as I wish I didn't. The same small nose, the dark hair, and the green eyes. Sometimes I wonder if it bothers my dad how much I look like her.

I was too little to remember her leaving. Too little to know how my dad was left broken and reeling from the shock of it all. He's told me stories, telling me she was his greatest heartbreak. When I was nine, I would ask him if he ever planned to find me a new mom.

The answer was always 'Not yet.'

As I got older, I realized he wasn't brave enough to tell me he would never remarry.

I climb the stairs and make my way to the bathroom so I can get ready for bed.

I brush my teeth, wash my face, and change into my pajamas. It's simple. It's the way I wish life would stay.

I climb into my bed, squeezing the life out of the teddy bear I have. It's the one Atlas gave me when we were ten and he won a game at the carnival.

One day I won't sleep with it. We'll both be older, wiser. I won't need a teddy bear to sleep.

But that time isn't here yet. Part of me wishes it would never come.

I drift off, dreaming of stars and constellations and wishes.

3

Atlas

THE BOOKSTORE STILL felt like her.

I shouldn't have gone in there. Priya looked at me like it pained her to even see me. Her tight voice, her attempts to be calm about my presence. But I could see the hurt in her eyes and the worry as she glanced to the back corner, then back at me.

Ophelia was there.

I considered for a moment walking back there and saying something. Anything.

Everything.

But doing that wouldn't fix us. Not with our last moment ending the way it did. With me walking away.

I take a glance at the fantasy section, the one we'd browse for hours in the summer, giving up the money we'd saved together and sharing a book.

I don't know how long I can take this.

"Do you need help finding something?" Priya had asked, her voice tight.

"No, I'm just... looking around."

But I couldn't stay. I couldn't breathe. I was out the door fast and walking away. I shouldn't have gone in there. But I wanted to remember what it felt like to be there. To be near her.

Ending up at Every Brew Café is probably the best decision I've made since returning to this town. The autumn air breezes past me as I sit on the patio, blowing crisp orange and brown leaves past my feet. I sip my coffee—black and bitter with just a little sugar to take the edge off.

I can still see the bookstore. See Ophelia when she walks out. I consider only for a moment going up to her. There's a longing in my heart, an emptiness in me that still seeks her presence. But the friendship we had is broken beyond repair.

I didn't think Ophelia would still live around here. I wouldn't have blamed her for getting away as fast as she could. I know I did.

But running away from my demons only complicated things more than it ever healed them.

The coffee isn't calming my nerves like it usually does. After downing what's left in my cup, I leave a tip tucked under the potted succulent on the outside table and walk down the street. Quiet is all that surrounds me, leaving me with too much space to think through everything. It's why I've taken so long to come back home. I've come to see my mom on holidays, but only ever for a day.

This is the first time I was brave enough to stay for the weekend. I didn't really want to be here this long, but my mom begged for me to come for a weekend stay. She said she missed me and wanted me home for a few days.

I didn't have the heart to tell her this wasn't my home anymore. I know she's lonely, ever since my parents got a divorce and my dad moved out of state. My older brother and his wife also live across state lines. I'm all my mother has, and I barely come here if I can avoid it.

My mom's house is tucked into the farthest part of the neighborhood, so I never had to worry about Ophelia finding me if I stepped outside. I never ventured farther into town on my one-day visits.

I don't know why I'm here now.

Maybe as punishment to myself.

I tuck my hands in my pockets, making my way down the street. Home is just around the corner. Although that's not too comforting when I know what will greet me. The look of pity on my mom's face because of my situation.

It's been a few years, I said to her when she started worrying. It's not like much has changed around here, anyway.

"I know…" she said, "but you only just came home again for longer than one day. I know it has to be hard on you."

Home.

I don't know if this is home.

I don't know if I *have* a home. This place reeks of death and loss. Grief permeates the air.

Two of the most important people in my life, ones I spent years with, gone in moments. And there's one I didn't give enough time to—to grieve or even consider.

Which is why it's all coming back to me now. Losing Ophelia was losing part of myself. But I was too caught up in my own emotions to realize that.

I find myself turning right before I reach my mom's neighborhood, heading towards the cemetery instead. I only visited her grave twice—once for the funeral and once before I left town. Yet I could find the place with my eyes closed.

The headstone looks as new as it did the day she was laid to rest. It does nothing to ease my mind to see the grave look fresh, almost as if this all happened yesterday and not five years ago. The vase is full of fake flowers, longer lasting than real ones. They're yellow and orange, the colors of the season. Her mom must've put them out recently. The sun hasn't faded them yet.

Her headstone is simple granite, the name bold and clear compared to the rest of the graves here. This is the newest one. Even in her death, it shows how young she was when she died.

Moriah Adams

2002–2018

"I should've made time to come by more," I say, as if she can hear me.

I kind of hope she can.

But the guilt in my heart doesn't really have to do with visiting the grave, or my lack of it. It has to do with what I should have done when all of this happened.

If I'd made better choices, maybe Moriah wouldn't be six feet under.

Sometimes I wish I could talk to her.

If she were still alive, though, I know we wouldn't be together. I probably wouldn't have kept contact, either.

She'd probably have some rich boyfriend who takes her on the European trips she talked about.

Yet, sometimes, I wish I could speak to her one more time.

Take back the things I said that caused all of this.

Prevent her from hurting me any further.

She wasn't perfect, like I used to think when we first started dating. Growing up without her has let me see the truth. She caused a lot of damage between me and Ophelia.

She also caused a lot of damage to me.

It took a while for me to see that I had changed into someone I didn't like when I was with Moriah. I was mean. Just like her.

For a long time, it was just Ophelia and me. We were united, unbreakable. And then Moriah moved to town. It became the three of us. It was like she had been the missing piece we didn't know about. My friendship with Ophelia was wonderful. But the three of us were perfect.

Or so I thought.

But then feelings got complicated... and the accident happened.

I couldn't stay in this town. I couldn't handle the reminders of both of them, knowing I was the one to break everything.

It was my words that made Moriah break.

It was my inaction that made Ophelia give up on me.

I couldn't be here, around the very town we all grew up in. Not after that.

Both of those girls deserved more from me. And now, neither of them is around for me to make things right.

I don't stay long. My heart can't bear it. I find myself walking to my childhood home, where my mom thankfully is not. Work probably has her tied up.

I decide to shower, to see if I can gather up some warmth where the world has left me cold.

I don't take long, though. I think too much in the shower.

After I get dressed, I find my mom has gotten home and is cooking in the kitchen. She gives me the same sad smile she always does and says, "I'm making your favorite soup. I thought you could use a nice meal before you drive back to your apartment tomorrow."

"Thanks," I say, coming up to hug her. She hugs me back, holding me tight.

We eat in comfortable silence. When I was a kid, we would always talk at the dinner table. Our conversations dimmed when my dad left. Eventually, this became normal.

Silence is all I can handle. I don't want to talk about what happened. It's been five years. I should be over it.

When darkness falls, I make my way to bed, even though I don't sleep until long after the rest of the world. I never can fall asleep. The calm and quiet of night brings up too much. And when I do finally drift off, my sleep is accompanied by night terrors.

I scream every time, which always brings my mom running into my room. She'll grab hold of me, pull me close, and let me cry on her shoulder until I wake up on my own. Otherwise, I'll claw at my face, at my hair, at my arms.

I shouldn't cry. I'm supposed to be the strong one, the man of the family.

Yet I can't seem to get a grip on myself.

"We should find a doctor," my mom suggests when I calm down from yet another episode.

"I'll be fine," I reply, like I always tell her. "I'm sorry for waking you."

Tonight, I don't fall back to sleep, despite the alarm clock on my bedside table blinking 3:30 a.m. But I pretend to sleep for Mom's sake. She'll be concerned and want me back on medication if I don't sleep on my own.

Sleep is for those who aren't haunted by the ghosts of the past or the demons of the present.

It's not for people like me.

I LOAD MY duffle bag into the passenger seat of my truck. My mom waits on the sidewalk for me. I shut the door and hug her. "I'm sorry I couldn't stay longer."

"I know it's hard for you to be here. And I know you're happy in the city, with your new friends. But remember that this will always be home, if you want it to be."

I reluctantly pull away from Mom, nodding slowly. "Always. I'll call you when I get to my apartment."

I don't look back when I get in my truck. I don't want to see her tears as I leave again. I never stay for long. I'm too scared to let the memories overcome me.

It rains when I'm driving home. I turn the heat up in the truck, but nothing will touch the chill that's overcome my heart.

Maybe I was hoping to say something to Ophelia, and that's why everything feels empty and pointless.

She'd hate me. Hate that I had come back. She'd probably have yelled at me for even being there. For entering her safest space.

I shake my head free of the thoughts. I don't want to linger on the memories. I focus on the rest of the drive, making mental notes of each recognizable place I pass. Tomorrow, I'll go back to work. I'll go back to pretending this part of my life never existed. It's easier in the city to drown out the noise in my head.

I pass by Darkest Night Bookstore, and for a moment I consider stopping one more time. One more opportunity to see her.

No.

I don't know what that would accomplish. I run a hand over my face as I leave the main area of town. I long to see her again, but I know she wants nothing to do with me.

I'm not even sure why, after all these years, I wanted to try.

Maybe I'm a glutton for punishment after all.

I drive straight through, stopping only once at a burger place to get something to eat. Three hours isn't a terribly long drive, but I blast the radio loudly, not letting myself get lost in thought.

The rest of the drive is easy. There isn't much traffic on a cold, rainy day like today.

I pull into the gated parking of the apartment,

sighing when I turn my truck off. Trips home remind me too much of what I've lost. I don't see my hometown: I see the things that no longer exist.

I don't see Carter's car in the parking lot as I walk to our apartment building. I climb the stairs to the third floor and unlock my door.

He's not home.

That's for the best. I can't handle his—or anyone's—concern for my wellbeing.

I drop my duffle bag in the living room, leaving my shoes on the rack by the door. I hang my coat in the closet, on my specific hook.

The walls start to close in.

Breathe in.

Breathe out.

Repeat.

I glance around the apartment, at the mess that has accumulated since I wasn't here to keep Carter on track.

Mind spinning, heart racing, I know that the only thing that's going to cure my never-ending emotions is to take back control.

Time to get to cleaning.

4

Atlas

Fifteen Years Old

THE SUMMER SKY is breathtaking in the evening. Pinks mixed with oranges and blue, like a painting.

I rock slowly back and forth on the park swings. Ophelia is sitting in the one next to me. She's silent, which typically means she's thinking about something.

"You don't have to be scared," I say, hoping to comfort her about the upcoming milestone. "High school really isn't scary."

"I'm not scared. I'm nervous."

"There's nothing to be nervous about. I'll be right there with you."

She leans her head on the metal chain that keeps the swing suspended in the air. "You're a whole grade ahead of me. I'll barely see you."

"You'll see me in the halls. You'll see me at lunch. I'll walk you to your classes when I can. And you already have a friend group waiting for you."

She shakes her head gently. "They're your friends. You're just letting me in because you're being nice."

I chuckle. "It's really not like that. We're not stuck up. Anyone can sit with us."

Ophelia sighs, looking up at the painted sky. "I feel like I'm standing on the edge of something that's going to shake up my entire life."

I lean back, then rock forward, letting the swing move a little more. "Sounds like a dramatic way to describe high school. It's not that serious. Unless you want it to be."

There's a moment of contemplation. Even though I'm trying to encourage her, I don't know if it's helping. The swing groans quietly.

Ophelia rises, sending her swing rocking. "I should head home."

I follow suit because I would never let her walk home alone. We walk side by side, in silence again.

I hook my arm through hers. "It's you and me against the world. I'm not going to let you suffer in school. Besides, we have a few more days before we start. We should try to do something big for the end of summer."

"Big? Like what?"

"Like getting a book and going to sit on our hill and reading it."

She laughs. "That's not big, Atlas. That's what we always do."

"We can make it a picnic."

She turns to me and grins, her eyes lighting up. "I'm sold."

I smile. "Then it's settled. Tomorrow, we'll go to the bookstore. You get to pick the book. I'll bring the food. We go up to our hill on the park, under the shady oak. And we hang out. One last little party before summer ends."

"Deal."

LUNCH CONSISTS OF only sandwiches, but neither of us cares. We eat the turkey-cheese sandwiches and take turns reading chapters of the epic fantasy Ophelia picked out when we stopped by the bookstore before coming here.

Moments like these are something I want to keep forever.

With my friends at school, it's different. We hang out outside of school. We have fun. But with Ophelia, I'm more relaxed. I don't have to worry about being something I'm not.

Things have always been comfortable here. Maybe it's because we're best friends. We've been inseparable since the day we met.

Ophelia glances up from the book, catching me looking at her. Her cheeks go pink. "What's wrong?"

It's my turn to be embarrassed. I rub the back of my neck. "I just wish everything could stay like this forever."

"You're sappy for a guy," she says, rolling her eyes. Still, she smiles.

"Only for you. I guess I was just thinking about everything."

She smirks. "Like you told me to stop doing yesterday?"

"That was about high school. I meant I was thinking about life. The future. I know I'm only a sophomore, but I know the moment I turn sixteen, the pressure will be so much more. College, sports—everything will become amplified."

"And I will be by your side." Her eyes light up when she says that. "We will never walk alone because we have each other. No matter what."

5

Rook

WORDS COULD NEVER describe how it feels to stroll back into my hometown in the dead of night. The place hasn't changed, not really.

The best part is how invisible I am, though I can't say even that is different from the way it was when I was here. Not many people dare to be out in the cold night. It's early October, but the chill is unseasonably severe for northern Texas. My human form would've hated it.

Thankfully, the weather doesn't affect me in the same way it once did. I can feel it, though, sense the way the wind shifts or the way it touches other people. The cold. The heat. I know it by the way it passes through me. But my shadow form doesn't change. I don't get hot or cold. I am existing only as a shadow, with no temperature.

None of it changes anything for me.

I casually stroll now, instead of floating around. I prefer the way my boots make contact with the ground I once trod upon as a teenager.

I can remember the route to my first target like the back of my hand.

Her house is dark for the night, save the soft glow of a lamp from somewhere inside. The lamp she leaves on for her father when he returns from his late shifts.

I have been an Umbra for a couple of years, but the one thing I have never gotten used to is the sensation of walking through walls.

The walls hate it, too. The house creaks slightly when I step through into its main hallway.

"Hush. I won't overstay my welcome."

I do hover above the ground as I float up the stairs. I doubt that creaky floorboard on the seventh step has been fixed, and I will not make more noise than necessary.

Her door is cracked, but I slip through as a shadow. She sleeps peacefully, unaware that I am about to enter her mind and create chaos in her nightmares.

It feels so perfect, like justice will finally be brought.

Do not forget your true goals, Rook. You are not here for petty revenge.

But I so desperately wish I could be. Alas, all I will do tonight is plant the seeds of destruction. I can't very well bring the chaos unless I set everything up.

"My darling Ophelia," I say softly, though there's really no need for that. She won't hear me. Not in the mortal realm. And she will not have access to the Shadow Realm yet.

I take a small orb from one of the many pockets I have on this suit. I crush it in my palm, then dip a finger into the liquid that remains and paint the blue juice onto her lips. Then a circle on her forehead.

She will feel none of it.

The blue juice is gone in seconds, planted somewhere in her mind.

"I will see you soon," I whisper.

This time, she hears, startling awake. I watch her look around, wondering what it was she might've heard. She can't see me. Her human eyes can't see beyond the visible. I may be but a passing shadow, a quick movement in the corner of her eye. But I don't exist beyond that. Not unless I want to.

And I don't. Not yet.

But soon I will. In the realm of nightmare.

I leave the same way I arrived. There's one more person I have to visit tonight here in town. I'm not entirely sure where she resides.

I find myself standing in front of the only coffee shop this town has, tracking the essence of the person I seek to find.

Reya, Ophelia's best friend. The one she attached herself to just before everything.

I find the essence and follow it to a house at the edge of town.

The walls of this house try to spit me out, but I persist. I find Reya asleep on the couch, a blanket tossed over her.

I pull out another blue fruit and crush it in my hand. When I paint it onto her lips, there's a shock that rides up through my entire being. She must be dreaming now.

Something about this one is wild. I don't know what it means that I feel the sensations of her dreams.

I shake my head. Perhaps Ophelia was not yet in a deep sleep.

I leave the house before it can expel me. That's two of my four targets.

I rise above the ground, taking flight to go to the city.

I've never been fond of the city lights or the way it never seems to rest. Cars still drive and people still lurk around as though it's not time for sleep.

Those who refuse to sleep at night don't contain dreams that we Umbra can feed upon. The dreams of the day don't quench our thirst.

I find Atlas and his roommate easily. Infecting them is similar to how I infected Ophelia. Neither of them is dreaming, so there's no shocking sensation.

I glance at Atlas one more time as I take my leave.

Soon I will have my revenge.

6
Ophelia

THE WIND ROARS in my ears, deafening. I'm freefalling, waiting, filled with a twisted acceptance that eventually I will hit the ground. Everything around me is dark. The night sky is a mild comfort. The stars are close enough to touch, yet my hands never seem to reach them.

I turn over, falling backwards. Above me, the moon is a haunting pale orb. When I right myself, the ground does not appear.

Instead, the ocean catches me in its cold arms, pulling me down. I see myself, further beneath the waves, drowning. I see someone swimming down towards me.

The next moment I see a graveyard full of fog and rain.

Then a pack of white wolves running through the woods. I writhe around in the water, the surface impossible to break through.

Then I wake up, gasping for air.

"All a dream," I mumble to myself, rubbing my eyes free of sleep.

I glance at the alarm clock on my bedside table. It's five a.m. I don't need to be up until seven, but my body always has a different plan.

I rise from my bed, knowing I won't fall back to sleep at this point. I grab some running clothes and take them to the bathroom.

After I finish my morning ritual, I make my way downstairs, slipping on my shoes. I'm silent, but then I remember my dad is on a business trip and there's no one else in the house to wake up.

I slip my earbuds in and leave, walking all the way over to the next street before I begin running.

Running is freedom.

It lets me forget things I wish would leave my memory forever. It brings closure and peace to an otherwise broken existence.

Priya says I'm insane for purposely running, but I crave the rush it gives me.

When I round back to the corner, I slow down and begin walking home. Letting the burn in my legs and my lungs fade. A quick stretch and one shower later, I'm gathering my things together to head to work.

I stop by Every Brew Café to get a ham and egg breakfast sandwich and two coffees—one for me and one for Priya.

It's still early when I arrive at Darkest Night, but I have a key. Priya comes out of the back room when she hears me.

"It's an hour before your shift. You need a hobby.

Maybe you could get back into writing poetry."

I offer up a coffee. "My hobby is bringing you coffee and lounging in the break room before my shift. Besides, my poems are trash."

She clicks her tongue and shakes her head, though she doesn't refuse her favorite latte. "They're not trash and I want to stock your future poetry book on my shelves, so I need you to please write again so we can make that happen."

I laugh. "That's a dream that will never be reality, but thank you for believing in me anyway."

I take a seat, Priya sitting across from me as she looks down at the book she's brought in. The break room is my favorite place in the entire bookstore. Priya has draped dark tapestries of the night sky on all four walls. Strung up around the ceiling and baseboards are fairy lights. All the lights in the room are warm and inviting. It matches the bookstore in the sense that it's decorated the same way. But there are plants in random corners, lockers for our things, and a coffee machine that we never use by the sink.

I sip my coffee and take a bite of my sandwich. Priya frowns into her cup as she takes another sip.

"Did I get the wrong one?" I know that's impossible. I've gotten Priya coffee for so long that there's no way I'd order wrong.

"No, no. I'm just... tired."

"I don't believe that's all."

She sighs. "Matthew wants money," she says, referring to her estranged husband.

"Do you have to give him any?"

She shakes her head. "According to my lawyer, no.

But he says he wants to get help. Therapy. And he's suggested couples' counseling. He says he's been living in his car for the past six months and can't get a job, which is why he's asking for money. But I… do I trust him?"

I don't know much about Priya's husband. I remember when they rolled into town, deciding this was the best place for their dream eccentric bookstore. I remember coming in every other Saturday with my allowance. Sometimes, he'd be organizing books or running the register. I didn't know at the time that something dark was going on.

I learned much later that addiction took away his ability to be the guy that Priya loved. Eventually, she kicked him out when she found he was stealing money from the safe to feed his cravings. From then on, she didn't talk about him.

And then I got old enough to work, and I knew this was the only place I could see myself working.

Now, she only brings him up when he's trying to get money, which has been once every few months since I've worked here.

"Do you love him?"

"I always will love him. Our vows aren't meaningless to me. And I don't think they're meaningless to him. In sickness and in health. But this is a sickness that neither of us knows how to fight. I don't want my money going to feed his addictions. I'm going to make a deal with him. He can come live with me—in my guest room—and we will go to therapy. If he needs something, I will buy it for him. But he is not going to touch any of my money."

"Did you tell your lawyer this?"

"I told her my plan. I didn't give her much of a chance to object, to be honest. But she has a concrete plan to help me evict him if I find out he's going behind my back in some way."

"That doesn't seem like a terrible idea," I say, sipping my coffee.

"I'm scared, though. I've missed him. I've wished he was by my side again, running the bookstore with me. Before he struggled, he supported my dreams. I know he loves me…" She falls silent for a moment. There are tears forming in her eyes. This has never been an easy subject for her.

"I know he supports me," she continues, her voice unwavering. "He's just struggling and I want to help him out of it."

I touch her hand. "I think you're doing the right thing, Priya. He's very lucky that you're patient and willing to help. I know if he truly loves you, he'll put the effort in for you."

She smiles softly, but I can see the doubt clouding her eyes. She stands up and throws her empty cup in the trash. "I'd better finish setting up the store. You take your time in here."

"Thanks."

When she leaves, I find myself pulling out my phone, going through the pictures I took years ago. Maybe it's the thought of Matthew coming back to town and trying to rekindle his marriage with Priya, or the longing for someone else who I think I saw yesterday. I scroll to the pictures that still sit in a folder on my phone, hidden at the bottom of the folders in my gallery. I've not had the strength to delete them.

Moriah, Atlas, and me, smiling as if we'd always be together. Me and Moriah, her dark hair and tan skin. Her smirk. Her quirks.

Atlas and his smile. His calm and peace. His forest eyes and messy hair.

Tears burn my eyes, threatening to overflow. I blink quickly, refusing to let them fall. I can't. I won't. Not here and not for him.

I rise, throwing away my sandwich wrapper and coffee cup. I will go out there, organize books, put on a strong face, and I will not let the memory of him haunt me today.

"OPHELIA?"

I look up to find Reya, the closest friend I have left in this town, standing in the doorway. We went to the same high school a few towns over, but never ran in the same circles. She was always with her group of eclectic people. I had Atlas and Moriah. Then I had Milo. But near the end, I had no one.

And that's when Reya found me. We've been close ever since.

She struts into the bookstore, a cold breeze pushing in with her. Her shoulder-length hair is a bright shade of pink, a contrast to the darkness in the room. Her hands are tucked into the pockets of her leather jacket.

"You'll never guess who was in the café yesterday."

My breath catches in my throat, and I know damn well that I wasn't making things up in my head. My heart knows, beats rapidly at the thought of him.

Him who I vowed to let go for good.

A ghost, haunting my town and my heart once again.

"Who?" The question is heavy on my tongue as I await the inevitable.

I don't want to know. I truly don't.

Priya glances up from her book, and I know my suspicions about the faceless voice are true. She saw him, too.

He did come inside yesterday.

And he was sitting at the café when I walked by.

"Atlas Jameson. I cannot believe he's back in town. I'm not going to lie to you; these five or so years gave him time to glow up. He didn't recognize me, but man, when I tell you there were at least a few of my coworkers staring at him like he walked off the pages of a magazine. His eyes—"

Priya clears her throat. Reya suddenly seems to remember who she's talking to. The girl whose heart was shattered by him.

"Right." Reya shakes her head and crosses her arms. "Atlas being hot isn't important. He shouldn't be hanging around town."

I shrug, rising from my seat on the floor where I was organizing middle-grade fiction. "I don't care if Atlas comes to town," I say defiantly. "His mom lives here. He has every right to visit her. I don't need everyone walking on eggshells around me. I'm not broken up about his existence."

Reya sighs. "You're the strongest person I know. You don't have to pretend like it doesn't hurt."

I look over at Priya. "I'm not hurt, and I know he came stumbling in here yesterday, too. I doubt he's in town for too long."

Reya shrugs. "I live a few houses down from his mom's house. I saw him leave this morning with his duffle bag. I assume he's already gone."

"Then why does it matter that he came into the coffee shop or into the bookstore?"

Priya sighs. "Because, Ophelia, we want to protect you and back you up. We both don't like what he did to you."

"And I don't like when the people I trust act like I'm going to fall apart any second. What happened was five—almost six—years ago. I'm fine."

It's enough to get them off my back. Enough for Reya to mumble something about calling me later as she leaves to go back to the coffee shop; her shift is likely starting soon. Enough for Priya to go back to the book she was reading in between customers.

But the lie lacks the conviction it needs to convince me.

Atlas was here.

And he didn't even try. Not to make an effort. Not to fix it. Not even to talk to me.

It isn't as though he should.

I'm nothing to him—was nothing to him for a long time before our friendship ended at Moriah's funeral.

But I can't deny that deep down, I've hoped every time he's come breezing back into town that he'd find me. He'd apologize.

He'd say something about this time and space between us.

I know it's foolish to want something I will never have.

Maybe the heart doesn't know how to let go of the first love. Something in me aches at even the mention of him.

"You're not okay," Priya says, sighing as she sets her book down on the counter.

"Of course not," I mutter, the hot tears stinging behind my eyes. I almost laugh at the idea of crying over Atlas again.

Almost.

But if I laugh, Priya will only think I'm crazy.

I cross my arms, willing my heart to stop aching from the memories. "I should be over it, yet here I stand, thinking of him being here."

Priya sits straighter. "Maybe he was looking for you. He looked... uncertain. Like there was something more to the visit than just browsing books. And he didn't really browse."

I shake my head. "He came because he has memories here, too. I don't own the town."

"His memories here are with you."

I turn back to the shelves. "I need to finish up the young adult section," I say, ignoring the flashbacks trying to take over my mind. I don't have the time or energy.

I need to let it go.

And now that he's left town again, likely until the next major holiday, it will be easy.

7

Atlas

I WAKE UP in the dead of night. At least I assume so, given how dark it still is. But as I try to turn over, I find I'm not in bed. I'm underwater. Gasping for air that won't come. Water fills my lungs. I'm going to drown here. *I'm going to die if I don't get out of here.* I thrash, trying to break the surface.

"You left me to drown You didn't try hard enough to stop me." Moriah's disembodied voice echoes through the depths of the ocean. "So now you will suffer the way I did." Though it doesn't sound quite like her soft tone. It's eerie, almost bitter.

I try to swim up, but I only sink further, vines of seaweed holding my ankles. My consciousness is slipping away, water taking over the last of my oxygen.

Then a hand pulls me up to the top. I cough up water, still not able to breathe. I am sprawled on a rocky beach, hacking up water, gasping, my lungs burning.

"Your pain is delicious," a mysterious voice hums from further up the shoreline.

When I'm finally able to take a breath, to gain the strength to hold my head up, I look towards the stranger watching me. He's floating in the air, his legs crossed. He's cloaked in darkness; his eyes are luminous white orbs. His face is shrouded in shadows. I try to move away, but I find myself paralyzed, floating once again with my head above water.

"W-who are you?"

"I am the mastermind behind this little nightmare. I am known by many names, but you can call me Rook. I know your deepest fears. Your worst mistakes. The things that make you guilty. Your pain is quite strong. It feeds my hunger."

"What?"

"There's not enough time to explain. You're soon to wake from all of this. Don't worry, Atlas. I will be back."

I shoot up, wide awake. Sweat trickles down my back, beads on my face, making my hair cling to my forehead and neck. I'm clutching my chest, gasping as if the air was truly taken from my lungs.

I've never been one to have wild dreams or even nightmares. But this felt like more than just a nightmare.

I run a hand over my face. It's obvious I'm not going back to sleep. I grab my phone from my nightstand, checking the time. Only 4:45 a.m. I shake my head. I have a few hours before I head to work. I turn my lamp on and grab the book from my bedside table. Might as well make use of the time.

WHEN I WANDER into the kitchen, Carter looks up from his bowl of cereal. "You look like a truck ran you over."

"Thanks," I mutter.

"Sorry I didn't get home until late. I met up with Rebecca after work and lost track of time."

I grab a cup to fill with water from the tap. "You don't have to be here when I'm here. You've got a life outside of me."

"Going back to your hometown never seems to do good things for you. And coming home to a spotless apartment and a roommate passed out on his bed doesn't feel great to me."

"I clean to cope."

Carter knows the darkest parts of my past. He knows why I blame myself for everything. It's why he knows the effect going home has on me. He doesn't usually ask questions.

But usually, whenever I get home, he's sitting up on the couch with the Xbox controller, ready to distract me until I no longer feel the pain gripping my heart, consuming my mind. Until it's no longer driving me insane.

It isn't too often I go into a cleaning frenzy, but when I do, I know it's a little intense.

"I know," he says slowly. "But if you need to talk about it, I'm willing to sit and listen."

I gulp down my water and say, "I'm actually going to get something to eat on my way to work. Thanks for the offer. If I need to talk, I'll tell you. See you later."

Carter nods, seeming unconvinced. But it doesn't

matter if he's convinced that I'm okay or not. I have to fake it till I make it.

Your pain is delicious.

My hand freezes on the door handle to my truck, the voice replaying in my head. They say people who show up in your dreams are people you've seen before, even if just for a glance.

But I would remember the glowing white of his eyes, the arrogance.

The poison of his presence.

I shake it off, pulling out of the parking lot and driving towards my job at the hardware store.

It was a nightmare, not unlike the many I've had over the course of the past few years. A night terror that gripped my heart and reminded me of everything I've lost.

I've had them many times.

But the memory of them never lingers this long. I always forget them. For some reason, though, this one is seared into my brain, which tells me there's more to it than just a simple mental disorder or a misfiring of my neurons during the night.

Maybe I'm being haunted.

Or maybe I'm making something out of nothing.

Even with my heart pounding and a small voice in the back of my mind telling me there's something more to the mysterious man who showed up in my dreams. The way he seemed to watch me, despite the pools of white seeming sightless in the shadows that obscured his face.

It was a nightmare.

Nothing more.

8

Atlas

Fifteen Years Old

THE FIRST DAY of my sophomore year. It's not as terrifying as the first day of freshman year. But there's still something unspoken that goes through everyone's mind. We've survived a year in the cutthroat place that is high school, but we're not done. We still have to survive another year to be considered something special. Only juniors and seniors have respect.

But I don't have to survive it alone anymore. Ophelia stands beside me in the parking lot where my mom dropped us off. It's her first day of freshman year.

"So," she says, watching as other students talk in little circles on the steps. "This is high school."

"Yeah. But don't worry. I'll be there to guide you

through everything. Us against the world."

We walk up to the entrance, and she smiles as I pull the door open, motioning for her to enter first.

The build-up to high school is a letdown. Ninth grade is no different than any other grade. Maybe it changes when you're a junior or a senior and you're at the top of the food chain in the unspoken hierarchy, but as freshmen and sophomores, we're unnoticeable.

I help Ophelia find her locker, leaning back against the one next to hers. I hear the hallway doors open, then heels clicking on the vinyl floor.

Ophelia says something to me, but my eyes have caught the source of the clicking.

It's a girl with dark raven hair and tanned skin. She wears a black skirt that falls just to her knees and a blue top that meets the waistband of the skirt. Her smile is one of confidence. As she gets closer, I see her eyes are brown, the warm kind that glows golden in the sunlight.

She might be the most beautiful girl I've seen.

"Who's that?" Ophelia asks.

"I don't know... but I'm definitely going to find out." I watch as the raven-haired girl continues down the hallway, my heart fluttering.

THE NEW GIRL walks into my English class, taking the seat in front of mine. The smell of her perfume invades my senses in all the best ways. My mouth goes slightly dry as she turns around in her seat, her eyes meeting mine.

"Hello," she says, and it's now that I notice the

reddish tint to her lips. "I'm Moriah."

"I'm Atlas," I say, returning her smile. "You're a sophomore? When I saw you in the hallway, I thought you had to be a senior."

She smirks. "You thought I was older? Everyone tends to think that. I like to present myself as more mature."

Class begins, but I'm so caught up in the smell of her perfume and the way her hair seems to fall in waves with ease that I hardly notice what the teacher is saying.

At lunch, I insist that Moriah sit with me and Ophelia. Ophelia is kind to Moriah, and we all start talking about our hobbies. Moriah likes to read, just like we do. But the books she talks about aren't ones I've really paid attention to. The popular books that trend online. The ones that everyone is reading. Ophelia and I tend to find the odd ones out in the bookstore. But now I'm tempted to look more into the books Moriah reads, given the way she talks about them.

She and Ophelia instantly seem to hit it off. I'm grateful for that.

As the week goes by, Moriah hangs out with us more and more, despite the cheerleaders trying to get her to hang out with them. I have no doubt Moriah will be a cheerleader when she's a junior.

Heck, I may even join a sport at that point, if only to stay close to her.

Moriah is bold and funny and smart. It's not long before I notice the butterflies in my stomach when she's around.

At night, I lie awake, thinking about her. About the smell of her perfume that seems to captivate a room. Or the way her eyes light up when she looks at me. Maybe she feels the same way about me.

I've noticed little glances in class, the small touches to my shoulder and arm. That's a sign, I think. Maybe she's feeling the butterflies, too.

I want to tell Ophelia, but I don't know if I should. We tell each other everything, but for the longest time it's only been us. Becoming a trio of friends has been nice. And since they get along, I don't have to worry about anything.

9

Ophelia

EXHAUSTION CREEPS INTO my body as I walk home. I don't usually feel so heavy after work, but the store was busy. Tourists from other cities often make the trip to Darkest Night. It's good that the store keeps busy in that way, but it's tiring as well.

Not to mention my mind lingering on someone I don't actually want to think about.

"Hey, Ophelia, wait up!"

I stop, turning to find Reya running up behind me. She's smiling as she slows by my side, looping her arm through mine. "You haven't responded to any of my texts today. I'm sorry if I upset you. I know I shouldn't have questioned your ability to cope with *he-who-shall-not-be-named* being in town."

"I'm okay." I smile, though I doubt it's convincing. "I'm just tired. It was busy today. And now I have to go home and figure out dinner."

"No worries." And she means it. Reya's been my friend since... well, since the accident. She knows when I need space and she knows when to check on me.

"Thank you for being so sweet, Reya. How about we go get dinner and catch up a little?"

"I would love to, but my family wants to have a family night. But we'll go soon, okay? You go home and rest."

I stop, hugging her. "Thanks, Rey."

I don't tell her that she was right all along, that my mind is lingering on Atlas. His voice, deeper than it has ever been, yet so familiar that I would know it anywhere.

I know he comes back to town for his mom every once in a while. But the fact that he stepped foot in my only safe space is frustrating. It's as if now that he's come so close again, I can't banish him from my mind.

Reya takes a turn at the corner, waving as she heads to her house. I enter my house, locking the door behind me. I eat some instant ramen and call it a night. My body is weary and craving rest.

I do my night routine, then slip into bed and let sleep overcome me.

A FOREST SURROUNDS me. But that isn't the most noticeable thing. Butterflies the color of night fly around, surrounding me. They're stunning and terrifying all at once. Dark wings of black and navy. They flutter about, some alighting on the trees, some lingering on the grass beneath my feet.

The other shocking detail is the ball gown I'm

clothed in. It's a deep plum and shimmers in the light. I wear no shoes, and there's a small blue pendant necklace hanging around my neck.

I wander through the woods, turning my head this way and that as I glance at the butterflies. They never touch me, instead parting in midair or lifting up from the grass, making way for me to walk.

"Ophelia?"

That voice.

I turn, despite telling myself not to look back at the inevitable.

Atlas stands tall in the clearing, butterflies surrounding him, too. They never touch him, either. His shirt is a blue button-up, though it's open. And his pants are dark slacks. His eyes meet mine, and there's something like warmth in the depths of them, like a current stirring in an ocean.

I shake my head. "I don't want to dream about you."

"This is a dream?" He seems confused.

"I would assume so. Why are you here? Never mind. My subconscious is clearly stuck on thinking you came into town the other day."

"I did. I was visiting my mom. I stopped by the bookstore, but I didn't see you. I thought it would be a long shot that you even still lived in town. But then I saw you walk out of the bookstore when I was getting coffee."

"I don't run away from tragedy and leave destruction in my wake," I bite back.

He frowns. "Ophelia... I don't think this is just a dream. I'm real. Or maybe you're in my dream."

"This is *my* dream. You're a figment of my imagination. One I don't particularly want to deal with right now."

I turn and keep walking, but he follows. He gently grabs my arm. "Ophelia, wait. Let me talk. This *has* to be my dream. All I did in town was think about you, so maybe my mind has conjured you up."

"That's not possible."

Dream Atlas is now getting on my nerves like real Atlas does. I wrench free from his grasp and continue pushing through the woods. Eventually I will wake up and he'll be gone.

I know he follows silently behind me. I ignore his presence, refusing to open up any more dialogue with a dream.

"Ophelia," he says.

I turn to tell him to leave me alone, but he's gone. Finally, my subconscious listened to me. I can feel my mind pulling out of the dream, the butterflies becoming blurry.

And then I'm waking up, tears streaming down my face.

10

Atlas

I SHOOT UP in bed. I wasn't ready to be cast from the dream. I wanted to tell Dream Ophelia how sorry I was.

I rub my eyes and go to stand, but that's when I stop. Surrounding my bed on the floor are dead butterflies, dark blue and black. I nearly scream at the sight, but instead I clutch my hand to my heart. I don't want to draw Carter's attention from down the hall.

I also don't want to answer any questions. All I know is I have to clean this up. I have to go see Ophelia. These butterflies prove that it was real.

That *she* was real.

I feel terrible trying to sweep up the butterflies. They feel sacred. But I gather them in the dustpan and empty them into my trash can, saving only one. It feels delicate in my hands. I set it on my desk while I slip into the bathroom to clean up before I get dressed.

I don't have work today, a rarity. So I should have

time to go back to the bookstore, to find Ophelia. I know she's there, and if she's not I'll wait. I have to speak to her and show her the butterfly. I may have missed her on my last visit, but I know she's still there, somewhere.

And when Ophelia left the bookstore, I know I saw her looking around, as if that invisible tether tying us together still existed.

As if she might have sensed that I was there, in her space.

I carefully wrap the butterfly in a tissue and put it in my backpack.

Carter is sitting in the living room, dressed for work. He has a bowl of cereal in hand as he watches TV. He looks up at me as I frantically slip on my shoes and my coat.

"Where's the fire?" he says.

I only glance at him for a second, unsure of what to say. I can't tell my roommate that a mysterious man visited my dreams, haunting my nightmares. And I certainly can't tell him I saw my ex-best friend in a dream, except we were real and I woke up with dead butterflies all over my room.

When I don't give an answer, he says, "You're off today. Usually you're still sleeping."

"I have to make a day trip back to my mom's house." The lie slips easily off my tongue. "I forgot something. But I'll be back this evening."

"Okay. Text if you end up staying the night. That way I'll know if I have the apartment to myself."

"I will."

I rush out to my truck, careful to place my backpack gently in the passenger seat.

Ophelia isn't going to want to see me, let alone talk to me. I know she will be furious that I'm even looking for her. But those butterflies in my room have to mean something.

The drive is quiet. I don't listen to music or a podcast. I don't make any stops along the way, like I usually do. Driving home isn't something I try to do in a quick trip. Even though it's a three-hour drive, I always drag it out, not really wanting to go home.

This time is different. And my heart beats faster and faster the closer I get. I decide to try Ophelia's house first. I don't know if she's at the bookstore yet, and it's still a bit early in the day.

I turn down her street, knowing the way her house by heart. There's one car in the driveway. Hers. My heart races with nerves; my stomach is in knots.

I rush to the door, ringing the doorbell. When there's no answer, I knock a few times.

The bookstore is within walking distance of her neighborhood, so my only other hope is that Ophelia walks to work sometimes. I'll try there, hoping that maybe Priya will have answers.

When I arrive at the bookstore, it's open. I park and make my way inside.

This time, it's not Priya behind the counter. It's Ophelia, helping a customer. When the customer walks away, I make my way closer.

"Ophelia?"

She turns to look at me, her face changing from an easy smile to a look of shock. I see the moment she closes herself off, the moment all emotion drains from her face.

There is no "happy to see me" after all these years. I knew that coming here would only bring her pain. But I didn't know that my heart would begin to rip from my chest from the way she looks at me now.

She tenses up, her hands gripping the counter. Her eyes, usually so full of hope and light, lose their luster as they settle on mine.

"Atlas..." she says, her voice choked. "What are you doing here?"

"I... came because I need to speak with you. It's important." My pulse pounds in my ears, blocking out all the sound around me. Music plays from the speakers, but I barely hear it. Books surround me, but all I see in front of me is Ophelia.

Like the dream. Except she's in normal attire, not the stunning purple ball gown she wore in the forest.

"I'm working right now. I don't think..." There's hesitation in her eyes. Despite every rotten emotion I know she feels about me, she's still Ophelia. She would not prevent me from telling her whatever it is I need to tell her.

"No." I step up to the counter. "Please. It's important."

"Can I help with something, Atlas?" Priya emerges from the back room. Her arms are crossed, but her eyes are sympathetic. She knows my past mistakes. And she's going to protect Ophelia at all costs. I don't expect anything less. But this is important to me and it's important to Ophelia, even if she doesn't know it yet.

"I need to speak to Ophelia privately. It's really important."

Priya studies my face for a moment, then looks to Ophelia. "You don't have to, but if you want to, I can watch the counter for a bit."

Ophelia bites her lip, looking at me with a mix of uncertainty and some other unidentifiable emotion.

She motions towards the back room. I look at Priya, who nods her permission. I step behind the counter and follow her to the small door in the back. Ophelia opens it, stepping inside and holding it for me. I brush past her, and a wave of regret hits me.

It didn't used to be like this. Accidental bumps. Arms intertwined as we took adventures through town. Never has it felt so cold to be this close.

The door falls shut and Ophelia stands at a distance. Her arms are crossed, her eyes studying the floor.

"I know you hate me," I begin. "And if this is all nothing, I'll leave you alone. But last night, I had this dream."

Ophelia looks up at me, her eyes searching mine. "You drove all the way here because of a dream?"

I nod slowly. "You were in it. We were in a dark forest and there were butterflies, dark as night, flying around."

Her eyes light up with recognition, but then she guards herself again. She forgets how easily I can still read her, after all these years. Her lips are downturned and her fingers tap on the table as if this is a waste of her time. I continue.

"I know this sounds crazy, but it was real. We both were sharing a dream. You can't lie to me and I can't lie to you."

"Atlas..."

"I know you were not some figment of my subconscious. We were sharing a dream. I have proof."

"Atlas, this all sounds a little insane. I get that obviously this dream really bothered you. But I don't know why you felt like I'm the person to talk to about it. People don't share dreams. Especially not when they haven't spoken to each other in years."

I flinch at that last part.

"I know I broke our friendship, Ophelia. I know I broke you, and I can never make it up to you. But please, give me the chance to prove to you that this happened."

I unzip the front pocket of my backpack and pull out the sacred cloth. I hold it out to her, needing her to take that first step. "Open it."

She looks hesitantly at the tissue in my hand, but slowly takes a step towards me, coming close enough to reach, but still so far away. Her fingertips brush my palm and another rush of guilt crashes into me.

She takes the tissue and holds it delicately in her palm. With her free hand, she opens it cautiously.

The black butterfly is still dead, but Ophelia's eyes are wide. Her face blanches.

"W-what are you doing with this?"

"When I woke up, a bunch of them were scattered around my bed. Feel the wings. It's real."

Tears glisten in her eyes. Maybe from the stress or from the impossibility of all of this. No matter what has happened, there is something connecting us. Her hands shake as she carefully wraps the tissue back up. I want to reach out to steady her, but I don't think the gesture would be welcome.

"So how… how is this possible?" Her voice shakes with the question.

"I don't know. But I do know something else. The other night, I had this nightmare. I was… I was drowning."

Despite the anger and the hate she has for me, I see her face soften. My hatred of being in the water is well known by those who have ever been close to me.

But Ophelia knows the truth about why I hate it.

"I was in some sort of ocean," I continue. "And I couldn't break the surface. Then a hand pulled me out, just far enough that I could see a man with dark eyes and a face shrouded in shadow. He told me my pain was delicious and that he'd be back."

Ophelia shivers, rubbing her arm. "So what do you think this means?"

"I'm going to sound insane."

"Butterflies from our dream—our *shared* dream— coming to life in the real world is insane, and yet it happened. You really think anything else is going to be more unbelievable than that?"

"Fair point. I think there's someone messing with people's dreams and nightmares. And I guess he's landed on me. And maybe even you."

She shakes her head. "The only person in my dreams has been you. I didn't realize it was really you."

"You still would've walked away," I say softly. "I deserve all the hate you have for me. Really, I do. I don't think I can ever forgive myself for abandoning you when you needed me most."

Ophelia quickly crosses her arms. Her eyes are glassy with tears she won't cry in front of me. Her lips are pressed tightly together, and I see this for what it is.

Anger. "I don't want to have this talk right now. It's four years late."

My heart clenches. She's absolutely right.

She hesitates, searching my eyes for something. I don't know if she finds it. "I don't know what to say about all of this. I don't know where to even begin."

She wraps her arms more tightly around herself; I can almost feel the anxiety seeping off her. I long to hold her in a hug and reassure her.

I almost do. But I stop my hand midway across the space between us.

"For now," I say softly, "I think we should document our dreams. You should keep an eye out for a mysterious figure."

She nods slowly. "If I see a strange man, I can tell you. In a text. Is your number still the same?"

"Yeah." I don't know if I should be surprised she's kept my number in her phone all this time, or relieved.

"If I see anything, I'll text you." There's an edge to her voice, the pain of this choice burning through both of us. "But for now, I have to get back to work. You should go home."

She hands me back the butterfly in its tissue cocoon, but I take Ophelia's hand and return the tissue and its precious cargo to her. "Keep this. I think it belongs to you."

Hope builds in my chest. Maybe this doesn't have to be so complicated anymore. Maybe there's forgiveness between us with this shared experience.

Our hands linger as my eyes search hers for any sign that we can be friends. But all I see are the walls built around her. Walls that I caused.

Without another word, I leave, my heart breaking all over again.

11

Atlas

THE PLAN IS in motion. I watch Atlas enter the bookstore. I sense one of the shadow butterflies in his backpack, but its life force is weak. It's almost dead, the magic nearly drained from its body.

But it has served its purpose by returning with him to the mortal realm. Seeing those butterflies in the dream and in reality has undoubtedly brought him here, to Darkest Night Bookstore. To Ophelia.

I hate to see such a beautiful use of shadow magic die in this way, but it's not unusual for other creatures made of shadow to cease existing the moment they enter the human world, even though their magic is enough to keep them intact.

I considered leaving the butterflies with Ophelia. But I knew she wouldn't think of telling Atlas. She didn't desire to reconnect the same way he did.

The dark shadows that took over the insects were

not just corruptible to my own whims, but deadly to the butterflies.

I wasn't sure if I could send something through a dream. Now that I know I can, there is so much more I can do to manipulate everything.

I consider entering the bookstore, spying on the conversation between Atlas and Ophelia. Maybe I crave the rejection that Ophelia will give him. I want to see him suffer the way I have.

But anticipation makes almost all things sweeter. There is a pleasure to be had in the chase, in the unknown. I am in control, but there is no need for them to know that. Might as well let them feel as if they're the ones controlling the situation, at least for now.

I fly over to the coffee shop to watch over Reya. She is a mystery that I've yet to unravel. While most people hold their fears somewhere in their subconscious, her mind is guarded.

I can't find the fears that shake her. All I've seen are vivid dreams of different times, things that seem far too real to be just her imagination.

But there is no fear lurking in the depths of her mind, which means I have to dig deeper to find what it is she's afraid of.

I study her closely. The way she ties her apron, the way she washes her hands so thoroughly. Her pink hair is in a short ponytail today, her lips painted a daring shade of purple. Something about her aura draws me to her. I don't understand how her mind is so locked away that my shadows can't reach its depths.

But I also don't want to drain her.

Wild energy like this is different.

My focus right now is on Atlas and Ophelia. They are the ones who've cast me into darkness, after all. I will seek my revenge on them. The butterflies are nothing compared to what I have prepared.

I soar away, landing on a rooftop at the edge of town.

"You're late."

I turn and stare at the interloper.

"Trig. What are you doing here?"

He's leaning against the stairwell door, surrounded by shadows, away from the sun. "The Council is getting a bit pissed about you, so, you know, one thing led to another. I'm keeping an eye on you."

"You mean spying on me?"

Trig is the shadow creature that stopped me from jumping off the bridge that dark and lonely night. He's the one I have to thank for simultaneously saving my life and condemning it to hell.

"Semantics, Rook. Tell me you have a plan besides following that pink haired-nymph around?"

I smirk, though I know he can't see. Umbra don't have faces. Not really. We have glowing eyes and that is all we see of each other. "Of course. She's one of my targets. Or she was, but her brain is locked tight. Bound by some sort of trauma, perhaps."

"A human mind isn't usually locked up. But I assume you have other targets for the quota?"

"Yes. Two."

Trig crosses his shadowy arms, pulling his cloak tighter around his shoulders. "Your quota is four."

I step closer, letting the sun pass through me. It

does not affect my shadows, nor does it prevent me from existing. It does render me invisible to the human eye. But Trig can still see me, is still tracking my steps closer to him as I come to stand beside him against the wall.

"My quota is understood. And I will drain four souls. But until I find two more, I'm working on the two that exist here. And I do have a plan. Tonight, I will cast them in a shared dream. The only escape will be to face their fears. And humans seldom take destiny like that into their own hands."

Trig doesn't seem convinced. His posture is rigid, his glowing eyes looking at me in what I assume to be disappointment.

"Humans will do anything to survive. Their hearts demand it."

"These are no ordinary fears. Tell the Shadow Council I will bring them four auras. They have nothing to fear."

Trig sighs, his arms falling to his sides. "I will be watching you closely, Rook. I have to. Please don't get yourself banished to the nothingness."

Trig is gone before I can blink. He has little faith in me. Sometimes I wonder what it is he saw in me that made him want to save me from the doom I had planned for myself.

I shake my head to clear it of these thoughts. Nothing about that matters now.

The game has only just begun.

12

Ophelia

IT DOESN'T MATTER how much time separates us. Atlas and I will always orbit each other. I watch him leave the bookstore yet again, his head down to avoid notice. His gaze almost broke me, the way he looked at me when I held the butterfly from our shared dream. I watch as he gets into his truck, the way he runs a hand through his hair, defeated. I will myself not to care. But there is always a piece of my heart that belongs with him.

"I see Atlas didn't quite get the reunion he was hoping for." Priya sighs as she leans against the doorjamb.

"You knew he came in the other day." I don't say it like a question, because it isn't.

"I saw him the other day. You were tucked into the kids' section, tidying up. I knew he was looking for you when his eyes didn't even linger on any of the books. I know he loves books almost as much as you do."

I don't smile, though the overwhelming urge to reminisce comes upon me. I remember summers lying in the grass in the park, reading one chapter of a book, then handing it to Atlas to read. Back and forth.

I remember the way the sun felt on my skin, the way his smile would warm me up on the inside. We were kids, but there was something special about the friendship we had forged.

He'd always keep the books, because I never had room in my home for them.

"They're memories," he would say.

I close my eyes.

"I'm sorry," Priya says softly. "I guess when he hasn't been around in so long, it's hard to face him, especially when your heart has just started to heal."

When people think of heartbreak, they think of star-crossed lovers falling from the sky they danced in. A tumultuous romance made of ups and downs. But for Atlas and me, that wouldn't be the case. It's far more complicated.

Priya clears her throat. "You know, today's been pretty slow. Why don't you take the rest of the day off? Grab a book from the clearance bin. I know you've been eyeing some of them. It's on the house. You need some book therapy."

I shake my head. "What I need is for Atlas Jameson to get out of town and go back to where he thought he was better off."

"First love hurts," she says gently.

"It wasn't love." Even the word tastes bitter on my tongue. "Because love doesn't leave the way he did."

I wander to the clearance bin, grabbing the small

paperback I've been eyeing for days. I go to the counter, refusing to leave. "I don't want to wander around feeling sorry for myself," I tell Priya, who is looking at me questioningly. "But I will sit here and read until it gets busy again."

"Okay," Priya relents. "I'll be in the back organizing the new shipment."

I open the book to the first page and start to read. I don't let my mind wander back to Atlas or the past. I don't want to remember when we were friends. Or even when I started wanting to be more. Because nothing will ever exist between us.

The bridge burned when he left me at my lowest point.

13

Ophelia

Fourteen Years Old

LUNCH HAS BECOME my least favorite time of the day. It wasn't so bad when I knew I'd have time with Atlas, time to talk about classes and ask him for advice since he's been through freshman year before.

I didn't mind Moriah, either. She seems nice, and we bonded over the fact that we are both new to this school. She also loves reading. Even though we don't read the same books, there is still an understanding between readers, a connection based on that shared pleasure.

But now, lunch has become the Moriah and Atlas show. They sit next to each other, giggling and talking about things that happened in their classes.

Sometimes it feels like I'm invisible, even when I'm right in front of them.

I take a sip of my water and glance around the

room. Everyone else looks like they have someone to talk to. Friendships have been forged already.

I'm left here, a third wheel to what appears to be something developing between Moriah and Atlas.

My heart clenches at the thought of it. Atlas and I have been friends for such a long time that the mild crush I have on him seems silly. I know it will lead to nothing. We're best friends and that is how it should be.

But every time Moriah touches his arm or his shoulder, or bites her bottom lip while listening to him talk, I want to flip the table. I want to stand up and demand they stop doing this in front of me.

It would be easier if I could hate Moriah, but she's too nice to hate. She's never been rude to me. Even when Atlas isn't around and it's just the two of us. She's exactly what I would've hoped for in a female best friend.

Yet she's stealing my best friend, my crush, right in front of my eyes.

There are only ten more minutes of lunch, but I can't take it anymore. I need to breathe.

I rise from the table, taking my tray over to the trash can and dumping my half-eaten lunch. I make my way to the nearest bathroom, hoping to hide in a stall so I can let out my tears.

My breath is shaky when I walk in, but there are other people in the bathroom, meaning I can't cry in peace.

I hate it here.

I walk over to one of the sinks and splash my face with water.

"You okay?" one of the girls I recognize from class asks me.

I nod. "Yeah, just feeling a little overheated."

Eventually I'm alone in the bathroom, but I only have two more minutes before the bell rings. I might as well get my stuff from my locker and get to class early.

Just as I finish drying my face, Moriah enters the bathroom.

"Ophelia, I've been looking for you. Have my texts not come through?"

I plaster a fake smile on and say, "Sorry, I guess my phone is on silent. I didn't realize. I'm about to head to class."

"I know something is wrong. You don't usually leave lunch without saying anything."

I clear my throat, willing the tears and the sobs to stay away. "I'm just tired."

"I know there's more to it. You looked sad at lunch."

So she *was* paying attention, but not enough to include me in their conversation. "Oh, it's nothing."

"I realized that I didn't talk much to you and neither did Atlas. Were you feeling left out? I'm sorry."

Why is she so perceptive? I feel the tears threatening again but I bite them back. I just want to get out of this bathroom, away from everyone. "No, no, you guys have a lot in common. It's all good."

"You'd tell me if I was overstepping in your friendship, right?" she asks, her eyes scanning mine.

She makes it impossible to hate her with how kind she is. Yet there's something nagging at me not to trust her.

"Of course. How would you be overstepping? We're all friends."

"Well, you've known Atlas for a long time. I would assume that maybe there's a little... more than friendship between you. And I realized that maybe I *am* overstepping."

I cannot have this conversation with her. I refuse to. "Atlas and I are strictly friends. The three of us are friends."

The bell rings, and I am grateful for my excuse to leave. "I need to get to class, but I appreciate you checking on me. I'm okay. Really." I brush past her and hurry down the hall.

I know she doesn't believe me, but I will not reveal how I feel about Atlas to someone I don't know well enough. She's nice right now, but there's something else I don't quite understand lurking beneath the surface.

Trusting people isn't something I'm good at. Not with how my life has been. But trusting Moriah feels like a huge mistake I'm not willing to make.

14

Atlas

I LIE AWAKE, staring at the ceiling. I should try to sleep. See if we meet in our dreams again. But after seeing Ophelia today, really seeing her, I can't get over everything that happened. Yet again, I'm wanting her to forgive me. To talk to me. To know it broke me, too.

But it's also my fault she hates me. It's my fault we're in this mess.

I roll to my side, facing the wall. Slowly, I drift off. I can tell I'm slipping into a dream world this time. Usually, it just happens. But my body starts to feel like it's floating.

Then I'm sitting on a rooftop, staring at the moon.

Constellations abound in the sky. None of them are in the right places, but they're there.

"Remember when we said it would stay like this forever?"

I turn to see Ophelia standing behind me.

"Are you real?"

She rolls her eyes. "You're the one that came charging into town today because you knew we were sharing dreams—literally—and now you're wondering if I'm a figment of your imagination?"

I rub the back of my neck. "Sorry. You're right."

She comes and sits beside me, leaving a gap big enough that I can't reach her.

The stars give a soft glow to the world beneath our feet, which looks so far away.

"I remember everything," I say. "I remember reading in the summer. Dinner. Constellations. Walking you home and thinking it wasn't fair you were all alone."

"Five years."

I look over to her, surprised to find she's staring right at me.

Her voice bites out the words. "You left for five years. You didn't check on me. You didn't reach out. You didn't even send a text. I know you had your own grief to get through. But you weren't the only one who lost someone when it all fell apart. And now you want to sit here and tell me that it wasn't fair that I was alone? You had left me alone long before Moriah died."

"I didn't mean it like that." Her words cut into my heart, tearing me to shreds. She's not talking about losing Moriah anymore. She's talking about me. "I messed up. I know I did."

"You did more than make a mistake, Atlas. You abandoned me in our darkest time. Moriah and I may not have been friends in the end, but I still cared."

I start to reach out, but Ophelia moves further away from me.

"Ah, a lover's quarrel. A delicious way to satisfy any appetite."

That voice...

A man shrouded in shadow appears, hovering above the ground behind me. I get to my feet and back up, blocking Ophelia from him.

"W-who is that?" she whispers near my shoulder. She is on her feet now too.

"That's the strange apparition I was telling you about."

"I'm hardly an apparition." The man seems offended. It's hard to tell with all the shadows. "Allow me to formally introduce myself. I am the mastermind behind these shared dreams. I also create chaos. You can call me Rook."

Black butterflies begin flitting about around us, never touching anything. But they fly regardless. One softly lands in Ophelia's hair. It lingers for only a moment before taking flight again.

One lands on Rook's shadowy arm. It seems to disturb the shadows warping around him.

Ophelia grips my arm. "We need to wake up."

"Oh, my sweet Ophelia," Rook says with a laugh. "You aren't going to wake up that easily. I have waited for this moment."

I stare at where his eyes should be, the luminous orbs soulless. The rest of his body is shadow, an essence of darkness floating off of him. "What do you want from us?"

"A little game is all I require. See, I have a desire to eat more than just the despair of the mind. I want to consume the very soul that resides inside each of you.

Your grief is powerful. However, I cannot just *take* you for my feast. I have to give you a fighting chance. Those are the rules."

"Rules?" Ophelia pushes my arm aside slightly to peer over at Rook. "What rules? And who decides the rules?"

Rook laughs. "I am an Umbra from the Shadow Realm, so to speak. Your grief calls, I answer. When a soul is grieved, it's poisoned with the emotion. All I do is come to eat dying souls the way a parasite comes to a dying animal. Your souls have grieved for so long that you hardly notice that they're decaying, waiting for someone like me to finish the job. As for who decides this... I'm sure you've heard of the laws of nature."

He crosses his legs as though he is seated, but he still hovers in the air. "The rules are if you can figure out how to escape the dream—rather, *nightmare*—I put you in, then you may keep your soul."

"What if we don't play?"

"You forfeit and I feast sooner."

I glance over at Ophelia. She's shaking, but her voice remains firm and unbreaking. "How do we know you won't betray us?"

"I'm bound to an oath. I can't physically betray you. If I even think of doing so, I will cease to exist. But there's no reason to doubt the one who has brought you here, trapped in the darkest parts of your minds."

He lazily leans back, as though reclined in a chair. All of this is a game to him.

None of this seems real. I'm nearly convinced this is a nightmare, one we've been forced to share. But I know deep down that's not what this is.

"We have to try," I say softly.

Ophelia doesn't move. Her eyes are fixated on the shadows that surround Rook. I turn back to him, ready to fight.

"We'll play your game. But we need something in return if we win."

He laughs. "You mean besides keeping your soul? You are in no position to bargain with me, human. You're lucky to hope you'll win against what I've designed for you."

I ignore him. "You have to promise never to haunt humans again." I shiver, despite trying to remain strong. This shadow creature has haunted my dreams and left me terrified to sleep. I don't want anyone else going through this. Not to mention the fact we're staring death in the face.

Ophelia seems tense next to me.

Rook almost seems to consider it, his silence the only thing giving any indication that he's thinking it over. "Unfortunately, I'm not sure it's possible to stop what I was created to do."

"I don't want anyone else to suffer at your hands," I say, sounding braver than I feel. "You have to vow you won't do this anymore. Since you can't lie, this should be simple."

He crosses his arms. "You aren't going to win, Atlas. So, I will accept your terms. Only because the pain will be so much sweeter when you fail."

"Fine," I say. Then let's do this."

15
Atlas

Fifteen Years Old

I KICK A rock, sending it a few feet down the road, the length of two whole houses. Moriah and Ophelia walk on either side of me. Moriah smirks as we pass the rock. "Might be a new record."

"You think so?" I'm hopeful she's impressed. Lately, things between us have been different. Subtle touches. Flirting.

As we've grown closer, I've realized how amazing Moriah is. She's super smart, always taking the advanced classes at school and joining in loads of extracurricular activities. She's also nice, funny, and she laughs at all my jokes. She makes me feel like the sun is always shining.

She laughs. "It could be. But is rock-kicking even a thing to break records for?"

"I could make it into something," I say slyly, giving her my most winning grin.

Ophelia breaks away from us. "I'm going to head home. I just remembered I have a lot of homework."

Moriah frowns. "So do we. But who cares right now?"

I can tell homework isn't the problem. Ophelia and I have a bond that's different. We can sense when something's wrong with the other.

I grab her wrist gently. "Are you sure? I can walk you home."

She shakes her head. "It's okay."

Her home is around the corner. I turn to Moriah. "I'll be right back."

Ophelia has already begun walking, but I catch up to her. "Hey," I say gently. "You can talk to me. But you also don't have to."

She doesn't say anything. Not at first. We reach her driveway and she turns to me. "Thanks for bringing me home."

"Ophelia... I know it's not about homework."

She doesn't meet my eyes. "Sometimes it *is* just about homework, Atlas."

"Yeah, but you're always ahead in school. Obviously, something is bothering you."

"I'm tired. Sometimes I miss when it was just the two of us. It's getting a bit exhausting keeping up with both of you. I'll be fine. Have fun with Moriah."

Before I can argue, Ophelia walks away, disappearing inside. I hesitate, not wanting things to end like that. But I don't want to leave Moriah waiting in the street for me.

I run back; Moriah's already gone. I look around.

Finally, I realize she probably didn't wait and headed to the snow cone stand without me.

By the time I arrive, she's holding two blue ones. "Figured I'd get here and order." She hands me the snow cone and we take a seat on one of the park benches. "Is Ophelia okay?"

"Oh, yeah. She really was stressed about homework," I lie. I don't want to tell Moriah what Ophelia said. Maybe to protect Moriah. Maybe to protect Ophelia.

"So, the spring dance is coming up," Moriah starts. "Have you considered who you're going to ask?"

I shrug. "I hadn't put much thought into it. I mean, I'll definitely be going. But I figured it would be with a group of my friends. What about you? Has anyone asked you yet?"

"Yeah, I've had a couple of guys ask, but not the one I'm hoping will ask me."

I take a taste of my snow cone. "Maybe you can ask him? I don't think that's a big deal. And honestly, I may just ask Ophelia. I've been through school dances before, but she may be a bit nervous."

Moriah nods, but there's a guarded look on her face. "That's true. I think it would look cute if you and Ophelia went together. You'd make a great couple."

I almost choke on my treat, which doesn't even seem possible. "Couple? I meant going as friends. You could join us, if you'd like. Ophelia's my best friend. I wouldn't be taking her as a romantic date."

Moriah shrugs. "It's pretty normal if friends catch feelings for each other."

"Yeah, of course. But that's not the case with me and Ophelia. I just wanted to support her through her first year at high school. It gets pretty rough when you're new to all the different things. And she's tough—don't get me wrong. But I also don't think I want to take a date to the dance. It's not that important to me."

I'm rambling, only because the concept of dating Ophelia has made me nervous. I've never really thought of Ophelia that way. I mean... maybe at times I've thought she was pretty. But it's never been much of a consistent thought in my mind.

If anything, I may be developing a crush on Moriah. But I definitely don't want to deal with that right now.

Moriah takes another lick of her snow cone. "Well, if you're sure, we can go as three friends. Makes it easier for me. It means I can dance with lots of guys."

"I thought you had a specific guy you wanted to go with?"

"Yeah, but I'm sure he'll be there. I can dance with him at some point."

She's so casual about the whole thing. I appreciate that it's not a big deal to her. "Okay. Then we'll go as friends. I'll tell Ophelia later."

I finish my snow cone first, but I wait for Moriah to finish hers. Then I walk her home. "I'll see you at school," she says with a smile.

As I walk back towards the street I need to take to head to my house, I turn the other way and go to the street Ophelia lives on.

I knock on her door and she answers, but instead of her usual smile, she looks tired. "What's up?"

Everything is awkward. Not half an hour ago,

Ophelia told me how she's tired of it being the three of us. And now I've gone and made a plan for all three of us to go as a friend group to the dance.

"Don't be mad at me."

"I'm not mad at you."

I shake my head, turning and taking a seat on the porch swing Ophelia's dad installed a long time ago.

Back when her mom was probably still around.

Ophelia sits next to me. "What's wrong?"

"I made plans for the three of us to go to the dance... after you said you're tired of it being the three of us."

Ophelia smiles. "Well, as long as you don't try to dance with both of us at the same time, I think I'll survive."

"I don't know. Maybe we can do ring around the rosy."

She laughs, but her smile fades quickly. "I've never been to a dance. I don't really know if I want to go at all."

"Well, I won't force you to go. But it would be fun if you could."

"I've had a few guys ask me to go, so I probably should make an appearance."

"Wait, you've been asked? I didn't even consider that. I should've talked with you first before making all these plans. Moriah..." I trail off. Sighing, I continue, "Moriah was saying the guy she really wanted to go with didn't ask her, so I was just trying to cheer her up. And of course, I had assumed you and I would be going together as friends."

Ophelia shrugs. "We probably would have made these plans at some point. It's okay. I didn't say yes to anyone. Not yet, anyway. That could change if I get a better offer than you." She grins slyly at me.

I pretend to be stabbed in the heart. "You've wounded me."

She laughs again, something I wish she'd do more often. Lately things have been too serious, with her nerves about school and always trying to stay ahead.

"You'll dance with me, right?" she asks softly, blushing.

"Of course I will. Moriah will definitely get many better offers than us while we're there. You're probably going to be stuck with me all night."

The thought of Moriah dancing with other guys stabs at my heart for real. But I have to be there for Ophelia more than anything. And I shouldn't care anymore what happens at the dance. It's just a stupid dance and doesn't mean anything.

I WALK INTO school early since soccer practice is before homeroom. As I head to my locker I see Trey, enemy number one. He's always trying to one-up me, despite being on the same team. We've both been in the running for team captain, but Trey has done everything he can to make me look bad.

I freeze when I see he's leaning next to Ophelia's locker, talking to her. She's smiling and... and laughing. She tucks a strand of hair behind her ears and there's a flush taking over her face.

I want to storm over there and push him away from her, but that wouldn't be appropriate. Ophelia can handle herself.

She knows I don't like Trey. She's probably just being polite.

I watch the conversation continue. When Ophelia hands Trey her phone, I realize he's putting his number in it. Why the heck does she need his number?

Trey walks away, waving to her. He's heading to soccer practice, same as me. I want to ask Ophelia what's going on, but she's heading off to the library before I finish closing my locker.

I get to practice on the field. Everyone is doing their warm-ups. I charge up to Trey and shove him.

He shoves me back. "What the hell, Atlas?"

"Why were you talking to Ophelia?"

His anger gives way to a smirk. "Wouldn't you like to know?"

I'm about to push him again, but Coach Rodgers blows the whistle, meaning we all have to line up.

Trey shoves me with his shoulder. "You can't hold claim on the two hottest girls in school, Atlas. It's not my fault you've been hoarding Moriah. If you cared so much about Ophelia, maybe you shouldn't have chosen the wrong girl."

I have no idea what he's talking about. I want to question him, but it's time for practice.

Ophelia and Moriah are both just my friends. I don't care if they date other people.

16

Ophelia

"BARGAINING WITH A shadow being isn't wise, but agreeing to the terms of a human is the most moronic thing I've done." Rook's voice is loud, as though it echoes in my head rather in this space. "It makes his risky behavior seem less stupid."

It's dark around me. It's like I'm floating in the night sky, but I'm not in outer space. There are no stars to light the way, or a moon to illuminate where I am.

Across from me is Rook, the shadow creature. Atlas is nowhere to be found. "Where am I?"

"This is the space between dreams and nightmares. Don't worry about Atlas. You'll be with him soon enough."

"Why am I here?"

"I wanted to speak with you personally. I've visited Atlas in his dreams before. I thought it was time I paid you a visit, too."

I cross my arms. "What do you want with me?"

He floats around in an orbit, circling me like a vulture. His gaze, or what I assume is his gaze, trails from my feet, up my body, resting on my eyes. "I'd hate to see you suffer. So I'm offering you a chance to escape. I could let you out now. It would be simple enough. Atlas can figure this out on his own."

"Why would you do that?" I can't believe it would be out of the kindness in his heart. I don't even know if these shadow creatures *have* hearts. His glowing orbs for eyes linger on me as he circles again slowly.

"Because, my sweet Ophelia," his voice whispers over my shoulder, his breath fanning my ear. A shiver rushes down my spine. Everything about him feels familiar, yet foreign at the same time. "You don't deserve what's coming to you. Atlas is dragging you down."

The thoughts swirl in my mind, his words playing to something inside of me. I shake my head, willing my own fears away.

Atlas chose to come see me after five years when the butterflies were in his room. And as if that weren't significant enough, sharing a dream seems like something I should pay attention to.

"I'm not going to leave," I tell Rook.

The shadow creature shakes his head, stopping his orbit in front of me. "Are you certain you want to help someone who has broken your heart countless times? What is there to gain? I'm giving you the opportunity to leave, to keep your soul intact."

The offer is tempting, for sure, but I think about Atlas, alone and fearful. I think about never seeing him again if he fails. He would die. And despite every terrible thing he's done to me, I don't want to see him suffer pain at the hands of this demon.

"I will fight by his side," I say firmly, my hands clenching into fists. My voice is full of false conviction. Atlas doesn't deserve for me to stay, but I'm not giving up before the game has begun. "I'm not abandoning him." I'm not sure why I'm defensive. But I won't abandon him to this nightmare. I refuse to. "Whatever test you're putting me through by doing this, you can end it. Send me to the nightmare."

Rook seems disappointed by my answer. I can't gather the ability to care. He stays in front of me for a long while, his gaze searing through my skin. One of his shadows reaches out, brushing my arm, then my cheek. It's warm, as though his hand has caressed my face in an act of reverence.

"So be it," he says softly, with an edge of bitterness. And then all goes dark again as I'm sent into a void, where all light and sound cease to exist.

My eyes flutter open. My back aches against something hard. It's not very bright out; the sky looks like it might rain. I roll over to my side, finding that I'm not alone.

Atlas is asleep beside me, though there are a few feet of space between us. I sit up, staring at him for a moment, wondering how long he's been asleep. Wondering if he knows where I've been. I rise to my feet, though the ground rocks back and forth. It takes me a minute to gather my bearings.

We're on a boat. I glance around, trying to make out where we are. The deck is wooden, like in the fantasy books. The more I glance around, the less tied to reality I feel. From the looks of it, this is a pirate ship.

Atlas moans from behind me, so I turn to see him sitting up, rubbing his eyes.

"What..." He looks around, coming to his senses faster than I did.

"What the hell? Where are we?" He's on his feet, rushing to the side of the boat, looking around.

"I would assume this is the nightmare."

"We need to wake up."

I cross my arms. "Oh, really? Why didn't I think of that? We woke up here, inside the dream. Tell me, have you ever woken up inside a dream?"

He turns, one hand still gripping the railing. "No," he says coolly. "We made a deal with the devil."

"So getting out of here means something more than just waking up. Rook said that much. We have to figure out the way to escape."

Atlas looks out to the water. His face pales, though his eyes harden as he glances at the ocean all around us.

I consider telling him what Rook offered me. The wind brushes against my hair, reminding me of all Rook said, of the way his shadows were warm against my skin.

My stomach churns as I watch Atlas; his face is taking on a green pallor. I know it's not sea-sickness, but rather the trauma that comes with losing someone to the water.

But I can't think about that now.

Rook's offer echoes again in my mind, this time faint. I wouldn't choose to make deals with the devil.

Atlas deserves to know what happened. He's been honest with me until this point.

I shake my head, deciding against it.

Besides, if he knows Rook kept me in a space between nightmares, offering me a way out... If I choose to fight by his side here, in this realm, he might think I've forgiven him.

I haven't even thought about forgiveness. If I'm honest, I don't know why I chose to stay here. I could be safe at home. I could be with my father.

But I know deep down, I'd be scared for Atlas, no matter how much he hurt me. I still care about him.

Which is why I'm here. It's why I'm concerned about him and his affinity with water. I know he hates being surrounded by it.

After the accident, I knew the water was his greatest fear. I knew he never went swimming again after what happened; summer came and he stopped showing up at the community pool. He'd been there almost every day, every summer before that, since he'd moved to town.

"Stop analyzing me," he says briskly. "Analyze the scenery. Help me figure out how to get the hell out of here."

"You're afraid to be known," I tell him, ignoring his directions. "Afraid that every rotten emotion you've kept inside will no longer be buried because you're stuck on a ship in the middle of the ocean with the one person who can read you like an open book even when you're a closed one."

Atlas grimaces, but I see his hands go from shaky to steady on the railing, fear giving way to anger.

"Stop."

It's one word, but it's so forceful that I comply. I turn away without a word, finding the door that leads below deck.

Fine, I'll study the ship. I'll look for something that seems like a way out. I won't talk to Atlas on this terrible boat where we're stuck. For who knows how long.

The boat goes up and down, but because this is a dream, I adapt quickly. I half-expect Atlas to follow me down here. To mutter an apology that seems insincere, but that I know is actually genuine.

But he doesn't.

And I don't want him to.

I descend the stairs to the deck below, but all I find are crates. Some are empty; some seem to hold corn. No rooms. Nowhere to sleep.

"Great," I mutter.

I search behind the crates, but there's not much to see. It's a typical fairy tale pirate ship. Most likely intended to keep us together.

I sigh, climbing to sit on one of the crates.

This is going to be a long night.

ATLAS WANDERS BELOW deck eventually and finds me sitting on the crate, where I've been for a while. His eyes are full of pain.

"Anything?" he asks, glancing around at the cargo.

"Not unless you want to eat a lot of corn, because that's all that's down here."

"How the hell do we get out of here?"

"I don't know. But lashing out at someone who

chose to stand by you isn't the way."

"What are you talking about? What do you mean you chose to stand by me?"

I seal my mouth shut, sliding down to the floor and walking past him. "Never mind."

He grabs my wrist, gentle but firm. "Ophelia, what did you mean? Did Rook say something to you?"

He's too perceptive. He's always been able to know what's going on in my mind, even when I've said nothing at all. I sigh, ignoring the fluttering as Atlas's hand lets go of my wrist and slides into my hand.

"I was caught between being awake and the nightmare. Rook offered me a way out. Some sort of back door. He said if I entered the dream, there would be no going back. That you could take care of yourself. I chose to come here." I yank my hand away. "I'm wondering if I should've let you deal with this yourself since you seem to like being alone."

I march up the stairs to find that it is now raining.

Great.

Fantastic.

"Ophelia," Atlas calls from the doorway of the stairs. "Come back. Please."

His voice is desperate. I'm tempted. Especially with the icy rain now chilling me to the bone. But I'm not sure if being stuck in a cabin below deck with Atlas is what I want right now. Too many questions with no answers.

I'm lost in thought, ignoring his voice, when my feet slide on the slick deck. I struggle to find balance, but it's no use. The surface is too slippery from the rain. I'm falling to the deck, my feet swept out from under me.

Two strong arms catch me, pulling me back away from the railing and into the doorway. Atlas is panting, still holding me with my back to his chest, his heartbeat racing against me.

"Don't...do...that...again."

I look behind me, into his face, finding fear mixed with anger in his eyes. "I'm sorry."

I pull away from his arms, though I find myself not wanting to. Not yet. I turn to face Atlas. His eyes are full of pain.

"Stop looking at me like I'm broken," he mutters. "I already know there's no fixing this."

"Fixing what? Us? Or your fear of water?"

"All of it, Ophelia. I know it's all over. It's only a matter of time before this nightmare kills us. That's the point."

"It may be the point, but it doesn't have to be the ending. There's more than one possible outcome to all of this. We just have to figure out the right steps."

I reach out, place my hand on his heart. It hammers under my palm, still racing. "But first, you have to be calm."

"Calm?"

He pushes away from the wall, coming closer to me. His eyes linger on my lips, then meet my eyes again. At first, I'm wondering what he intends to do. But then he starts down the stairs. "Might as well make ourselves at home, then," he calls over his shoulder. "We're going to be here a while."

I exhale, unsure what all of that was. I glance out at the rain. There is a flash of lightning, and then a peal of thunder rumbles, shaking the ship. I follow Atlas down below.

17

Ophelia

Fourteen Years Old

MORIAH GROANS. "WHAT should I wear?"

"A dress."

"Ha ha ha, you're so funny. I meant between these two options."

I roll over to my stomach on her bed. On her laptop, she presents two dress options. A lavender cocktail dress that looks like it belongs on someone going to a club, and a sky-blue dress that is, thankfully, a little longer.

"You're pretty tall, so the purple one would probably be a little risky for homecoming."

"I want to be risky. I want to stand out. I want Atlas to look at me and think I'm pretty."

My stomach twists itself in knots. "Aren't you going as friends?"

I know it shouldn't matter to me. I'm going with

Trey. But Trey agreed to go with me as friends. I have no intention of trying to get a boyfriend by the end of the night.

And selfishly, I had hoped that maybe it would make Atlas jealous. Although that clearly didn't work.

"Yes, I know," Moriah says, sighing. "But I want to dance with him. I want…"

I sit up, letting my book fall to my lap. I'm realizing that this dance isn't going to be the fun friend bonding experience that Atlas has painted it as. Moriah wants to impress him, which means she wants something more to come out of this night than just a dance.

She wants to walk out of there with a boyfriend.

I swallow my pain and rise from the bed. "I think you should go with the sky-blue one, but you make the final decision. It is your birthday money you're spending." I gather my stuff. "I forgot I have some homework left, so I should get home. But I'll see you tomorrow."

She gives me an odd look. "You always say you have homework. I'm starting to think you don't want to hang out with me."

"No, it's not that. I just… am a bit behind on school. I have to catch up." The lie rolls off my tongue easily. I've been using it as an excuse to get away from anything having to do with Moriah and Atlas growing closer and closer.

I don't like pushing Moriah or Atlas away, but I can't talk about my issues with them. Not when it involves them.

Moriah sets her laptop aside, crossing her arms against her chest. "Ophelia, just tell me what's up. I know you're hiding something."

A shiver runs up my spine despite the fact it's not that cold in Moriah's room. My hand is resting on her bedroom doorknob, my escape so close I can touch it.

Yet she's starting to see through my lies. I exhale slowly. "Do you like Atlas?"

"Of course I like Atlas! We're all friends, aren't we?"

I shake my head. "I didn't mean like that. I meant do you *like* Atlas?"

Moriah seems to consider my question. "I don't know. I thought you had a crush on him."

My face flushes. "What? He's my best friend. I don't—"

Moriah giggles lightly. "Ophelia, I'm not stupid. I see how you look at him longingly. I watch how you two interact. I thought he was *your* territory."

Something doesn't add up. There's her words, but there's also the flirting banter. The not-so-innocent touches on his arms or hands. If she thought I wanted to date Atlas, why would she do those things? Something gnaws at me from the inside out.

Do I trust her with my longest-kept secret?

"Well?" she asks impatiently. "Do you have a crush on him or no?"

"I... no."

No.

I shouldn't trust her. Not with this. Yet somehow it feels like I've hammered the final nail into the coffin. Something about the finality of the word "no" strikes me.

"Ophelia, you've never been a good liar."

"What?"

Moriah sighs, rolling her eyes. "Your nose twitches

slightly when you try to lie. Emphasis on the word *try*. You're not good at lying. I can always tell. So do you want to tell me why you're scared to admit you like Atlas? I mean, you're best friends. I think developing feelings is perfectly normal."

"It's not... I don't..." It's no use. "Fine. Yes. I've liked Atlas since I was thirteen. But it doesn't matter. He's my best friend, and that's important to me. Feelings can come and go."

Moriah smiles. "I'm not trying to get Atlas to like me, if that's what you're worried about. We're all friends here."

Something tells me there's more to it than that. Is she the one lying now?

"I'm serious about the homework," I say, finally opening her bedroom door.

Okay," she says, her focus returning to her laptop and the lavender dress on the screen. The one that will show off her curves and her legs. "I'll see you later."

I leave her house without another word, heading around the corner to my house.

I catch sight of Atlas, out for his usual jog. Soccer season is coming up and Atlas has played since he was younger. He jogs daily to keep up his endurance. I quickly pick up my pace, hoping he doesn't see me. He'll know with one look at me that something isn't right. I don't want to confess my feelings and I don't want to think about the confession that was forced out of me moments ago.

"Ophelia, wait up."

I keep walking, pretending not to hear. He's still a couple of hundred yards behind me, so I can easily pass it off as not hearing him if he asks later.

"Ophelia, what's wrong?" His voice is near now, not something I can ignore. I stop walking and turn, finding he's caught up. He's next to me now, panting. His face is flushed from the workout or maybe from the sun. It's hard to know for sure. His dark hair clings to his forehead.

"Why did you keep walking?"

"Oh, sorry. I must not have heard you the first time."

I wonder if my nose twitches. I wonder if he knows about that. He seems to believe me, though. Maybe I can get myself out of this conversation quickly.

"It's okay," he sighs, still catching his breath. "What are you doing over here?"

"Oh, nothing. I was just helping Moriah with something, but I have a ton of homework."

"I can walk you home."

"You're jogging. It's okay. I don't need an escort all the time, you know."

He smiles. "I know, but I wanted to talk to you about homecoming. I saw you talking to Trey."

I tense up slightly. I was talking to Trey to be nice, but when he asked me to homecoming, I felt like maybe I should I have some insurance, an alternative to going with Atlas and Moriah and feeling like a third wheel. "What about him?"

"He's taking you to homecoming. He's my soccer rival. So, I guess... I don't know. It seems weird."

Of course, this is the conversation I wanted to have. But not in the context I wished for. This is not going to plan at all.

"It just kind of happened," I say, feeling flustered. "He wanted to ask me. And besides, I told you I might accept another offer if I got one."

"So Trey is a better offer than me?"

I shake my head. "It's not that, Atlas. He's not 'better.' I'm going with him because he seems really interested. Besides, you'll have Moriah."

I add that last part, wondering if it's true. Wondering if he feels the same thing about her as she feels about him.

"I had hoped all three of us would go together, though."

"I didn't want to feel like a third wheel, Atlas. It's so obvious that you and Moriah aren't just friends anymore. And until you figure it out, it's just too hard for me to be around the two of you."

Atlas's eyes widen. "What are you talking about?"

"Come on. You like her. She likes you. Where does that leave me? It leaves me trailing behind like a lost cause. You're going to the dance with Moriah. You agreed to go with her. That's basically a date. So what's the problem if *I* got a date to the dance?"

"Um…nothing." He shakes his head, running a hand through his dark hair. "There isn't a problem. But I agreed to go with both of you. As friends. I didn't know you wanted to go with a date."

I didn't want to go with a date. I wanted to go with him. I resist the urge to shake him and scream. "It'll be better this way," I say calmly. "Besides, now you can just focus on Moriah, which both of you want."

"I… what? I mean… Okay." He sighs. "If this is what you want."

"Good. I'll see you at school tomorrow."

I continue on my way before he can argue with me further. I want to be alone, and I'm hoping he realizes that.

I'm not far when I hear his footfalls catching up

behind me. He keeps up with my stride. "It's you and me against the world, remember?"

I shake my head, keeping my gaze forward. "Not this time. Moriah... really wants to impress you. And I think you should have the opportunity to go to the dance with a real date."

Atlas is silent for a moment, but I know he's still following behind me. I finally stop, turning to look at him again. His mind is working overtime, according to the look of pure focus on his face. He's trying to figure everything out and come up with a simple solution. Except nothing will be simple about this situation.

"Just have fun with Moriah," I tell him.

He grabs my wrist gently, something he always does when he feels untethered from everything around him. I force my eyes to meet his, even though it hurts to think that after tomorrow, I'm going to lose my best friend.

My crush.

"I won't force you to go with us," he says. "But I would hate not to have you with me. Just promise to save me a dance?"

"Are you sure Moriah won't mind?"

"You are my best friend. I don't care if she minds it or not. I'm not her boyfriend. She doesn't decide what I do. Please?"

I nod, because I'm at a loss for words. This seems to appease him.

"I'm still walking you the rest of the way home," he says softly, letting go of my wrist slowly.

"I know," I say, barely above a whisper.

18

Atlas

I STAND IN the center of the ship, as far from the water as I can get. The skies remain dark, but the rain has eased for now.

I came up in the night, unable to sleep with the rocking of the boat. All I could think of was the ocean around me.

Ophelia comes to stand beside me, not breaking the silence. She wanders to the railing, looking out at the water.

"It's violent, the way the waves crash against the ship."

"That's why I'm here in the center of the deck. I can't breathe below deck, and I'm fairly certain I'll die up here, too. But that doesn't seem to matter."

She glances back at me. "The point of this isn't to be easy. We have to figure out what we're missing in all of this."

Nothing is missing. But I don't say it. I close my eyes, feeling the rise and fall of the ship beneath my feet. I used to like being on boats, out on the water. Swimming, jet skis, wakeboarding—I soaked it all in. I've even dabbled in surfing.

But now, I can't even bring myself to look at the ocean without seeing the way Moriah looked when she was pulled from the water. Her skin a pale green, her hair matted to her face.

I take a deep breath, too untethered to open my eyes.

The waves rock the boat violently. I stumble over my feet, lurching to my knees on the deck. Lightning sizzles, and a clap of thunder crashes in the air. My eyes fly open at the sound, and I see another lightning flash in the distance. I'm paralyzed. A hand grabs my shoulder, breaking me from the moment. Ophelia looks as afraid as I feel. "We need to get below deck," she says near my ear.

Rain starts to fall, a few drops at first, then a full-on downpour. We begin to run towards the stairs, but the ship starts to rock as the waves crash violently against the hull.

I'm unsteady on my feet; the deck is slick with rain. Ophelia grabs my arm, trying to steady herself. Her hands are cold against my skin. I can only imagine how cold I must feel to her.

The stairs feel far away, like the storm is blowing us backwards across the deck. I nearly slip again, but Ophelia grabs my arm, guiding me to the doorway.

"We shouldn't run," Ophelia shouts over the downpour. "We'll just slip and fall."

I nod an agreement, taking each step carefully. She releases my arm, walking cautiously behind me. It's tedious and painful. The rain has thoroughly soaked me now and my teeth are chattering.

Finally, the doorway is within reach. I grab the wooden paneling and turn to face Ophelia. I reach out my hand, back into the rain, something she can grab onto. Just as her fingertips brush mine, a massive wave crashes roughly against the ship.

The force of the water causes the ship to jerk wildly. Ophelia slips on the deck. I go to grab her hand, but I'm slipping, too. I grasp at a metal pole nearby that is rooted firmly into the deck. This holds me steady despite the rocking of the ship. With my footing firm, I reach out again to Ophelia, who is only a few feet away, trying to rise from all fours. Our hands meet, and I grip hers tightly, despite the slick rain on our palms.

We steady ourselves, fighting against the wind and the rain. Carefully, we make it back to the stairs. I usher Ophelia in first, then follow her.

The ship rights itself, but it continues to rock viciously in the storm. Nothing about this feels real. I guess the magic of the dream is working against us.

"I don't know how to get out of this." Ophelia exhales, her clothes clinging to her body. She's pacing, rubbing her arms with her hands.

I pull my soaked shirt off, laying it on one of the crates.

"You have a tattoo?"

I stiffen, unsure why I feel suddenly vulnerable with Ophelia here. "Yeah," I manage to say.

She steps closer to study my back. Down my spine

is a series of birds in flight, etched into my skin in black ink. She doesn't touch them, though something inside of me wishes she would. I want to feel her cold fingers against my spine. I can almost feel her gaze burning hot on each bird.

"It's nice." I feel her breath on my back. I turn to face her, finding she is closer than I thought. "Is it real or is it just the dream?"

"It's real. I got it a couple of years ago."

She nods, and then her eyes fall on the tattoo on the front of my left shoulder. It's a compass. This one she says nothing about.

"Remember that book we read when we were young that I hated because the main character died in the end?"

"Of course," she says softly.

"I read it after the accident. I saw it on my shelf. I needed to have something tangible to hold onto. And I finally understood the ending after all these years. So I got a compass tattoo like the main character had."

"What does it mean to you?"

"Hope. I may not know True North now. But I want to find it."

Maybe I have found it, at this moment. Looking at Ophelia, I realize that my path has always led to her, even when we both wanted to be far away from each other.

I made a lot of mistakes in my heartache. I pushed away the one person who has never judged me for all the things I've done wrong.

I was afraid to find out if I had been wrong about Moriah.

I was afraid to let my mind wonder what would've happened if I had made the right choice.

Neither of us speaks for a while, but I can feel when Ophelia glances at me. Studying me.

"So, what do we do?" I break the silence.

"I don't know." She doesn't move back. "The only thing I can think of is trying to take control of the ship. But we need to wait for the storm to die down for that."

"There has to be a way to wake ourselves up."

"I don't think so. He seemed pretty determined that we had to *do* something in order to wake up. But I don't know what that would be."

"If it has to do with fear… maybe we have to take control of the ship while it rains." I hate myself for even bringing a voice to that thought.

She shivers, finally moving away from me. I grab my wet shirt and say, "I'll try to do it. You stay here."

"No, we should go together."

"It's dangerous."

"That's the point. We both have to fight to wake up. So, we both have to face the danger head on."

I nod slowly, though I don't like putting her in any more danger than I already have. The ship is still rocking violently, but we slowly climb the stairs. My shoulders hit the side wall a few times; it's hard to keep my balance against the angry storm.

We both pause when we reach the top. The rain is heavier than it ever was, the ship tilting and turning in the gale. The deck is slippery. As we step into the rain, the ship tilts violently. Ophelia loses her balance and slips sideways.

"Ophelia!" I reach for her hand, but find myself

sliding, too. I catch the railing, bringing myself to a stop.

Ophelia slips over the short railing and falls overboard.

"NO!" I yell, as she disappears beneath the waves. I wait for a breath.

Then two.

When she doesn't break the surface, I know there's no time to hesitate.

No time to think.

I close my eyes and let go of the railing. I plunge into the icy the water, letting the waves crash above me.

I choke when water rushes down my throat, my arms and legs flailing. Panic claws at my heart, my chest tightening from the cold and the fear. I break the surface for only a second, barely catching my breath. I need to focus. Ophelia doesn't have a lot of time if she's underwater. I swim around, looking for any sign of her in the murky ocean.

I dive.

I can hardly see anything, trying to hold my breath as I look for her.

I break the surface again, though this time the waters are doing everything they can to keep me down. I gasp for air, taking it in, then dive again.

I'm starting to panic when I finally spot her. She's sinking slowly, not fighting the water.

She's unconscious. And there's a cut bleeding on her temple.

I swim fast towards her without a second thought, grabbing her around her waist and bringing her to the surface. I work to keep her head above water, to keep her from slipping away from me. I'm battling hard enough to keep myself above the waves.

"Ophelia," I yell over the howling wind.

She doesn't respond. Her eyes don't even twitch. I don't know how much water she took into her lungs. And that cut is bleeding worse now that the water can't wash it out.

My right arm is tight around her waist. The other arm keeps us afloat as I tread the water.

The storm is not letting up. I try to head towards the boat, but I don't know how we'll get back on. As I get closer, I realize that, in the violence of the storm, a life preserver must've been knocked off the boat. It bobs on its rope, a circle of orange beckoning to us from near the railing. I swim towards that, though it takes forever battling the choppy waves and dragging Ophelia, whose weight is only increasing as my arms tire.

That scares me, makes me wonder if she's even breathing. I have to get her to the life preserver, use it to hold her up. Then I can try to get us back on the boat.

I pull the white and orange ring over Ophelia's head, threading her arms through. It holds her up as her head slumps to the side. I push my fingers to her neck and can feel her pulse throbbing weakly against my fingertips. It's very faint, but still, it's enough to make me hopeful.

I start to look for a way back onto the boat. I push the life preserver toward the hull, keeping a hold on it to help me stay afloat as well.

There are hand- and footholds on the side of the ship, but of course Ophelia can't grasp them.

Not in her condition.

The choice is clear: save myself, or doom us both.

That's when I notice a small dinghy that hangs near the railing of the ship. Somehow, in the chaos, it wasn't knocked free. If I can bring it down, I can get us both to safety.

"I'll be back. I promise. Please don't let go," I murmur next to Ophelia's ear, brushing my lips against her cheek before I climb to get the dinghy.

I keep an eye on Ophelia; the waves are making her rise and fall. But thankfully, the orange ring continues to hold her firmly, although her head is still slumped.

I climb into the dinghy and begin lowering it to the water with the pulley system.

Once I'm down to the surface, I jump back into the water to push Ophelia's life preserver closer. I then haul myself back into the small boat and pull Ophelia inside. I lay her down on the small bench, waiting to see if she'll wake up on her own.

I check her pulse once more. It beats stronger than it was before.

"Ophelia," I murmur, but my eyes begin to shut. I'm exhausted. My body slumps against the other bench.

Then everything fades away and it all goes dark.

19

Atlas

Fifteen Years Old

"OH, HONEY, YOU look great!" My mom is beaming at me as I stand by the stairs in my suit for homecoming.

"I can't wait to see what Ophelia's dress looks like."

"What about Moriah?"

My mom's smile softens a bit at the edges, but she nods. "Of course. I'm excited to see hers, too."

My mom is driving us to the homecoming dance. I was a bit hesitant, unsure if she would embarrass me in front of Moriah.

I never have to worry about those things with Ophelia. Ophelia knows every embarrassing thing about me. But Moriah...

I straighten my bow tie and follow my mom out the door to the car. Ophelia is already waiting.

"I thought I would walk over," she explains. "Since my dad couldn't be home to see me."

Her dress is stunning. It's simple, coral with gold accents on the top. Her hair is done up on her head. And she's wearing makeup, which isn't something she often does.

It looks good on her.

"You look amazing," I say.

She smiles warmly. "You clean up pretty nicely yourself." Her smile falters a bit. "Moriah will be very impressed."

I shrug. "I don't care about being impressive."

It's a lie. I absolutely care. That's why when I asked Moriah what color her dress was going to be, I got a purple bow tie to match.

We load up in the car, and my mom drives towards Moriah's house. I sit in the back with Ophelia. When we get to Moriah's house, her parents are already outside taking pictures.

And her dress is... shorter than I expected. It is many inches above the knees, showing off her very tanned legs. She's done her makeup in purple, and her hair is falling in ringlets down her back.

We all step out of the car. My mom introduces herself to Moriah's parents. I've met them a few times before. While they talk, I walk up to Moriah. "You look great," I say. And I do mean it. But the dress itself excites and terrifies me. Its plunging neckline is a bit startling. She looks hot, but I'm not really used to seeing girls dress so... sexy.

I've never cared much for what people wear, but this dress seems a bit out of place for a school dance. "Aren't you worried you'll get cold?"

Moriah smiles brightly. "I'm not concerned about

that. We'll be inside all night. Besides, we'll be dancing, so it will be fine."

"Atlas, let's get a picture," Moriah's mom says.

I pose for a few pictures. Ophelia stands by my mom, and I wave her over.

"Oh yes," Mrs. Rodriguez says. "Ophelia, you should get in the pictures, too."

Ophelia walks over, though I can tell something has changed in the vibe around us.

After pictures, my mom drives us over to the school, dropping us off at the front. We're about ten minutes late. The dance has already begun.

"Behave, use manners, don't go off with anyone you don't know. And call me when you're ready to come home," she reminds us.

After she leaves, Trey finds his way over to us, taking Ophelia's hand. "There you are. I was waiting for you to show up before I went inside."

"Sorry, we were getting pictures. I should've asked for you to come by."

"It's okay. My stepmom took a crazy amount of me and my sister anyway. Ready to dance?"

Ophelia follows Trey inside. Moriah grabs onto my arm and leans her head on my shoulder. "Let's have fun," she says softly.

Walking into the gymnasium is nothing new for me, but I'm amazed at how great everything looks, better than my first dance last year.

Banners hang on the wall behind the sound stage. There are streamers of purple and blue hanging from the ceiling. Tables off to the corner hold snacks and fruit punch. I notice a couple sneak off under the bleachers, away from the watchful eyes of the teachers playing chaperone.

Moriah twirls around. "It's not exactly how my old school used to do things, but this is very nice."

Moriah comes from a richer city up north, where the school was much more refined and fancier. This is probably nothing compared to the dances her school would put on. But she seems happy.

We dance, we jump around, we drink punch, and we eat cookies. It's fun. Everything is going amazingly.

Eventually, Moriah says, "I need to go to the restroom. Maybe find Ophelia so she can give you that dance she promised you?"

"Okay."

I look around for Ophelia, but I don't see her. I assume she's with Trey. I push through the crowd of people, squinting against the strobe lights flashing to the beat of the loud music.

I look around, finding Trey by the punch table but no sign of Ophelia. In fact, Trey is cozying up to a different girl in a red dress.

I head off in a different direction, wondering where Ophelia might be. The gym is crowded and loud. If I know her, she's probably somewhere fewer people are.

I finally find her sitting behind the bleachers, crying her eyes out.

"Ophelia?"

"Atlas." She sniffles. "I'm sorry. I just needed a moment."

"What happened?" I ask.

"I made a fool of myself thinking Trey was

anything but the jerk you warned me he was. He told me he thought I was cute and he asked me on a date. I accepted. But then he disappeared, supposedly to use the restroom. And then I found him making out with Heather Chang in the hall. He was playing me."

I pull Ophelia into my arms as she sobs. "I'm so sorry," I say softly, running my hand up and down her back in an attempt to comfort her.

She sniffles and clears her throat. "It shouldn't matter, honestly. I didn't come here with him expecting a date. I came because I didn't want to be a stupid third wheel."

"You're not a third wheel. It's you and me against the world. Always and forever."

Ophelia shakes her head. "I'm just going to walk home."

I shake my head, pulling her in for another hug. "You promised me a dance."

"I don't feel like dancing anymore."

"Okay, well, you can at least come hang out with me. You promised you'd hang out with me a little bit. Who cares about Trey, anyway? In a week, it will be some other girl he's messing with and Heather will be a thing of the past. That's how he is."

"Okay…" She's hesitant. But I pull her to her feet and lead her out to the dance floor.

"Come on. I've waited all night to dance with you."

20
Ophelia

WHEN I OPEN my eyes, I'm no longer sinking in the water. It takes me a moment to get my bearings. I'm not in my room, and the mattress beneath me is softer than my own. An arm is slung over my waist. I turn my head slightly to find Atlas next to me.

This must be his room. For a moment, I lean into his chest, letting him hold me.

I remember falling into the water. I remember how it felt to lose air, to lose consciousness. I thought everything was over.

It was dark and cold.

Yet here, in his bed, I'm warm.

I'm alive.

I'm not frightened that we woke up in his room, but it's strange considering I didn't fall asleep here. Maybe the same magic that brought the butterflies here brought me here, too.

Atlas gasps suddenly, squeezing me to him in his sleep. "*Ophelia.*"

I touch his arm gently. "I'm right here."

His eyes flutter open; his breathing becomes sharp. He sees me and seems to realize where we are.

He relaxes, his hold loosening. "How... what..."

I roll onto my back. "I don't know. I don't know what happened after I fell into the water. I couldn't see anything. I thought I was drowning."

"You were," he says. "I dove in and grabbed you. I was able to get us to the dinghy that was attached to the boat. But there was a lot of work to do. After that, everything faded and I—we—woke up here."

"You...dove in after me?" I know about his fear of water. After losing Moriah, I know he didn't ever go near water again.

"Of course I did. I don't... I won't let anything hurt you. I've lost you once, and that's something I'll never forgive myself for. I can't lose you again."

A rush of heat flushes my cheeks. Atlas lies on his back again, staring up at the ceiling. "How did you end up in my room, though?"

"I guess I followed you from the dream. Like the butterflies followed you."

He sighs. "My roommate is going to be so confused when we come out together."

I laugh slightly, knowing this will definitely look pretty suspicious.

Suddenly, Atlas's alarm is going off to my right. I grimace at the sound. But in the next moment, all oxygen escapes my body. Atlas rolls over towards me, leaning over me to turn it off. He's propped himself up above me, on his elbow.

I shift under his arm. "I could've turned it off, you know. You didn't have to roll on top of me."

"Well, you *are* on my side of the bed," he says with a smirk.

I look up at him as he goes to move back down. But our eyes meet and he freezes above me, his face near mine. His eyes gaze down at my lips. He reaches one hand to my temple, brushes his fingers there. They linger, as do his eyes. For a moment, I think he might kiss me.

I find myself hoping for a moment that he will.

But then he's moving away, and the warmth that flooded my face is fading.

"I'll take you home," he says easily.

I should be angry that I'm here, in his bed. I should be upset that he has to drive me home, three hours away.

Yet something has changed between us. He jumped in the water without thinking. He did everything he could to rescue me, despite having everything working against him. Despite the storm and every instinct he had screaming at him, telling not to.

He saved me.

He faced his fear of the water to bring us both back alive.

That's it!

I shoot up. "I figured it out!"

He sits up beside me. "Figured out what?"

"You jumped into the ocean to save me. You didn't hesitate or think about your fear of water. You dove in and you pulled me back up to the surface. And then we woke up. You faced your fear."

He stares at me for a moment, considering. "So

Rook is putting us in trials where we have to face our worst fears?"

I nod emphatically.

"So now, when we fall asleep tonight, we'll be teleported again?"

"Maybe... I don't know if it will happen again. I mean... we're back here. We passed that test. Would he really send us back to another dream?"

I glance over at the alarm clock on his bedside table. I'm beyond late for work.

"Crap," I mutter.

I search for my phone, which I find in my pocket. I'm still dressed in yesterday's clothes. Somehow in all the chaos, my phone is untouched. Maybe the dream didn't really have an effect on anything in the waking world.

Just on our spirits, our souls.

I see about a dozen texts and three missed calls from Priya. I call her immediately.

"There you are, my friend. Are you okay?"

"I overslept. I had a rough night. I'm so sorry."

"Don't worry. We aren't busy. I can handle it today. You take the day to relax."

"No," I shake my head, though she can't see me. But then I realize I'm three hours away. By the time I'm back home, my shift will have about thirty minutes left. There's really no point.

"I'm serious, Ophelia. You work very hard. Take today to rest."

"Okay." I feel absolutely awful for doing this to her. "Thank you, Priya. I owe you one."

"You owe me nothing, sweet girl." She pauses.

"Maybe a coffee, though." She laughs slightly.

"A thousand coffees. I'd better go. Thanks again."

I hang up, turning back to Atlas. "Priya gave me the day off, so if you have work today, you can just take me home after. I don't want to interfere any more than I have."

"No. I was off work today. I have all the time in the world for you." He bites his lip, a quirk he has when he's thinking.

His words make me shiver. I quickly sit up and swing my feet to the floor, then stand up.

"Well," Atlas says, stretching his arms above him. "I'm hungry. Why don't I take you out to eat and then we'll get you home."

I smile. "Okay. I *will* let you take me to breakfast."

He gets out of bed. "Just let me get changed so my roommate doesn't ask more questions than necessary."

"And if he does ask questions?"

"He knows about you. So I'll tell him as much as I can. You needed a place to crash or something."

He told his roommate about me?

Before I have time to question that, he's disappeared down the hall with a fresh set of clothes. I sit on the bed, waiting.

When Atlas returns, he says, "We're in luck. Carter isn't here. So let's go get food and then get you home. I'm sure your dad is wondering where you are."

"He hasn't even noticed I'm gone," I say with a shrug. "Today isn't one of his off days, so right now, he's still asleep after his night shift. I usually see him on his day off, and then in passing when he gets home. He's usually about to go to bed when I'm getting up. He probably thinks I'm at work when he gets home and

I'm not there."

He won't notice I'm gone, and for once, that works in my favor.

Atlas's expression is unreadable. I know how he feels about my dad never being home. He always made it clear when we were younger that he didn't like me being home by myself.

Times might be different, but some things never change.

I follow Atlas through the apartment to the door. He grabs his keys and his coat, which he puts over my shoulders.

I shiver when I step outside, though it's hardly the chill in the air.

It's the fact that I no longer hate Atlas Jameson. And every old emotion is stirring up inside of me. Unwanted and unnecessary.

Yet I don't want it to stop.

21
Ophelia

Fourteen Years Old

NOTHING ABOUT HOMECOMING is special or fun or the party that Atlas was promising it would be. There are older kids sneaking off to make out in the corners of the room where the adults aren't paying attention. I roll my eyes and ignore the sight of it.

Music fills the room, not too loud, but not quiet either. Lights flash, and people sway and dance.

And with my date using me as a dare, as someone to make fun of behind my back, I'm pretty much over the entire high school experience that is homecoming.

I'm not having fun.

Atlas bumps his hip to mine, swaying gently next to me. His smile is wider than I've ever seen it. "Come on and dance."

I shake my head. He takes my hand gently and tugs me towards the dance floor.

For a moment, I can forget that he's here to be with Moriah. I can go back to believing that it's me and him against the world, like he always promises.

I ignore how my heartbeat races at his touch because I don't want to think of how I have a crush on my best friend. I just want to remember what it was like to be best friends.

That's all I want tonight.

So I let go for the length of the song. I dance with Atlas, letting him spin me away and pull me close to the beat of the song. Moriah is nowhere to be found. She wouldn't care. She doesn't see me as a threat. She knows Atlas and I have been best friends and there's nothing that changes that.

Then the music slows. Couples start pulling each other close, swaying to the music.

"You should go find Moriah," I say, pulling away from Atlas. "You've paid me a lot of attention tonight."

He tugs me back towards him with his hands on my waist, pulling me into a hug and swaying with me. "She'll be okay. I want to make sure you're having fun."

"But what about her?"

"I've spent half the night dancing with her. Besides, she's been dancing with some other guys and keeping herself busy. And I promised I would make sure you didn't regret tonight. Besides... you're my best friend."

He's right... and he's also wrong. I'm hoping he doesn't feel the way my heart is racing against my chest, threatening to break free. Or the way my hands shake slightly behind his neck.

This is everything I've wanted. Yet it's not what I want at all. To know his heart belongs somewhere else while his arms are around me is a cruel joke.

As the music fades, I hold him tighter, trying not to cry.

He rubs my back. "You and me against the world. Always and forever."

His words are a whisper in my ear.

I only wish I could believe him.

AS WE LEAVE the dance and get into Mrs. Jameson's car, I wonder if I can believe him. Maybe there is truth to his promise.

Atlas sits in the backseat with Moriah while I sit up front with Mrs. Jameson.

I ignore the fact that Atlas and Moriah are whispering and giggling. I glance back, though I instantly regret it when I see Moriah has her hand in his. Maybe it's friendly, but something in my heart says it's more than that.

But Moriah was so insistent that she knew I had feelings for Atlas. She also said she wasn't trying to be with him. So what is all this? Could it really be that she's just touchy and they're talking?

But my heart drops to my stomach when Atlas walks Moriah to her door, and she leans in and kisses his cheek. I look away, knowing that if I keep looking, I'll break.

Atlas returns to his seat in the back, talking with his mom as they drive me home. He tells her about the dance and doesn't ever ask me to fill in any details. I appreciate that very much. Mrs. Jameson pretends she didn't see Moriah kiss his cheek on the front porch.

I pretend, too.

When they drop me off, I thank Mrs. Jameson for bringing me home. I tell Atlas a quick goodbye before he can get out and walk me to my door. I race up to my house before the tears can break free.

My dad is home tonight, for once. One of his coworkers needed to switch shifts with him, so he had a normal day of work and was home in the evening. He also wanted to be home for my first dance, in case I needed him to come get me.

"How was it, Ophelia? Did you have fun?"

Fun. Of all the words to describe that experience, that isn't one I would use.

"Yeah, it was alright. I don't know if I liked it."

I hated it. Maybe not the part where Atlas comforted me. Or the part where we danced. But everything after that shattered my entire experience.

Moriah accuses me to my face of lying about having feelings for Atlas, then kisses him anyway.

Yeah, it was just a kiss on the cheek, but it still meant something to both of them. And now all I want to do is scream and cry.

My dad tilts his head. "Are you okay?"

"I'm tired. That was an exhausting experience. I'm going to shower and go to bed."

"Okay, bug. But you can talk to me if something's bothering you. I'm sorry I'm never here."

I understand why he's never here. I don't resent him for it. My mom made a lot of money and when she dipped out of our lives, he had to do something. And everything he's doing is a sacrifice to keep us here, in the house I grew up in. I never complain about him being gone, although I miss him constantly.

When I say nothing, my dad pulls me into his arms and I finally break down and sob. He doesn't make me say what's wrong. He doesn't force me to speak through the tears. He just holds me close until I'm numb enough to stop crying.

Afterwards, I take a shower and clean the night off of my body.

I knew Atlas didn't reciprocate my feelings, but Moriah knew better. And that's what breaks me apart inside.

When I'm finally in my room, ready to sleep everything away, my phone goes off. I don't look at it, not immediately. I don't want to linger on my emotions. And when I see Atlas has texted me his usual goodnight, I don't reply. I know he'll ask what's wrong tomorrow.

But tonight, I can't face him.

22

Atlas

OPHELIA WAKING UP in my bed was strange. Yet I can't dismiss how natural it felt to be beside her. Or how right it feels that she sits in the passenger seat of my truck right now, looking out at the city as we drive.

I should never have left her behind. I should've been there for her. I can't help but wish I had been a different person when I was seventeen.

I wish I had been able to see who Ophelia was to me the entire time, instead of wasting time with someone who didn't truly love me the way I loved her.

I run a hand through my hair, trying to bring myself out of the memories. I don't know how to start a conversation with Ophelia like I used to. Before, it was always so easy. Now I don't know how to keep her comfortable. The silence is slightly unnerving.

"Do you like the city?" Ophelia asks softly, looking at me as I drive.

"Sometimes. The chaos and the noise keep me distracted."

"What are you wanting to be distracted from?"

The question is so innocent and simple, but it catches me completely off guard. I stop at a red light, my hands falling from the steering wheel.

"I guess... our past. I've made a lot of mistakes."

When the light turns green, I make a left turn.

"Where are we going?" Ophelia asks.

"Breakfast. You can't leave this city without trying the best diner you'll ever visit."

"Better than Every Brew Café?"

I laugh. "This isn't a café. This is a diner. Therefore, you can't make me choose which one is better."

Ophelia laughs too, and I realize how much I've missed that sound.

How much I've missed her.

When I park, I quickly hop out and rush to the other side to open her door.

"Wow, it looks like the city has taught you some manners." There's a smirk tugging at her lips as she looks up at me. A rush of heat floods my face, though I'm not entirely sure why.

"I've been well-mannered my entire life, thank you very much. Now tell me, are waffles still the best breakfast food?"

She elbows me. "Absolutely."

"Then you're going to love what this diner has to offer."

"I will be the judge of that," she said, her eyes alight with hope. Despite everything we've just been through, I take a breath and look around. Something about this diner, something about the city, feels a bit like home. The rush of traffic outside. The 50s theme inside.

Stuck in time, many would say.

The waitress wear poofy skirts that hit above their knees, and their hair bounces in ponytails and red headbands.

It's my favorite place to be when I need to get away from the world.

But right now, the weight of the world sits on my chest.

I almost lost Ophelia a matter of hours ago. Something inside me is wanting to protect her at all costs.

I guide her to a booth near the back, by a window. The cloudy, rainy weather is somehow the perfect atmosphere for the diner.

A smiley waitress bounces over to the table. "Welcome to Last Stop Diner. What drinks can I get you started with?"

Ophelia smiles softly. "I'll just take a glass of water."

"I'll take a lemonade, please," I say.

The waitress writes it down, then sets two menus down in front of us. "I will be right back with your drinks."

Ophelia opens her menu, but I playfully take it from her. "You have to have the waffles."

"Maybe I want to explore my options." She smiles mischievously.

"Trust me, that's the only option for a day like today."

She playfully rolls her eyes but releases the menu

from her grasp. The waitress returns with our drinks and I order two of the waffle stack plates.

I watch as Ophelia stares out the window, watching the cars drive by on the busy road. The silence between us is comfortable. I don't want to break it yet. I want to take in every flicker of movement, every breath she takes.

I want to feel every heartbeat, remember that she's still here, she's alive. I wasted time thinking love was behind me.

It's right in front of me.

Ophelia turns to me and grins. "You're staring hard. I might start to think you care about me if you keep looking at me like that."

"I do care about you. I think I've proved that."

Her forest green eyes meet mine. "You have. More than proved it. Thank you."

I'm about to say something I may very well regret when the waitress returns with two plates stacked with three waffles each.

"If you two need anything else, just let me know."

"Thank you," I say as she retreats to another table.

Ophelia stares at the waffles, then immediately begins applying butter and syrup. "Time to see if you're right about these waffles."

I wait as she takes her fork to cut off a bite of the top waffle. Her eyes close, and a look of pure enjoyment spreads over her face.

"Okay." She relents with a sigh and opens her eyes again. "You win."

I smirk. "I told you I knew what I was talking about."

The rest of the meal is silent as we eat our waffles and watch the world go by outside.

"Does it ever get overwhelming?" Ophelia asks as we walk back to my truck.

"What?"

"The city. The busy streets. The people who stare right through you."

I shrug, opening her door for her. I make my way around to my side and slide in, turning the key in the ignition. "I find it overwhelming being home, where everyone knows my business and they don't know how to stay out of it. I go home to visit my mom, whom I love dearly. But I find myself getting pitiful looks from Ms. Davis down the street or Mr. Turner as he eats at the café."

"You went through something unimaginable, though."

I lean back in my seat. "Maybe it's harsh of me, but Moriah and I would've been over before high school ended. If she survived that trip to the beach, we would've broken up. I wanted to break up with her." I pause. This revelation is something I've never really acknowledged out loud. I probably look as startled as I feel.

"Obviously, I hate how everything went down, and I do miss her. She was my friend before she was my girlfriend. But it wasn't all sunshine and happiness. Even though everyone else seemed to think it was destiny."

Ophelia looks over at me, her eyes studying my face. "You were going to break up with her?"

"Yes. We had a fight before she got in the water. I was actually going to get my mom to come get me to take me home. But then the storm came, and Moriah…"

Ophelia touches my arm, and I can't ignore the way it makes me feel to have her here with me again. To know she cares about how I feel.

This whole twisted circus with Rook, the nightmare wielder, has been nothing short of crazy. But it's brought me back to her.

We're not yet the best of friends again, but maybe we can be.

I stare at her, studying the way her eyes search mine. Savoring the way she bites her bottom lip as she thinks of what to say.

I've always been frustrated when people get stumped on their words and treat me like some kind of grieving boyfriend who lost his soulmate.

But I don't feel that with Ophelia.

"Even if you didn't feel the same love for her that you did when you started dating, it was still traumatic," she says finally. "And you still grieved."

"And in that grief, I did the one thing I promised never to do. And I have never regretted anything more."

There's a new intensity between us now. A bond forming that can't be broken. We almost died in a nightmare and woke up in the same bed.

It would take less than a second to pull Ophelia in right now and kiss her. Every fiber of my being wants to.

But there are wounds I have caused that I have yet to fix.

"I should probably start driving or else your dad will worry."

"I doubt that," she sighs, leaning away to look out

the window. "He still works a lot."

The atmosphere is different on the drive home. It's not bad, but we barely speak. I turn the radio on low. A soft pop song is playing. I think it's about love and loss. I should change it, but I find myself leaving the station on as I put the car in gear and the clouds give way to light rain.

OPHELIA'S HOUSE IS exactly the way I remember it. The bushes line the railing of the front porch. The windows are dark and shuttered.

"Thanks for bringing me home," she says. "Would you like to come inside for a few? Stretch your legs from the drive?"

I desperately want to spend more time with her. I want to talk about so much with her. Lingering here is sounding better and better by the moment.

But then my mom might learn I'm back in town and start to question what's going on. I don't know if I have the bandwidth to explain any of this, least of all the evil shadow demon who's wanting to eat my soul and haunting my nightmares.

Besides, I have work tomorrow.

"I want to. But I need to get back on the road."

She nods. "Okay. Call me when you make it back, okay?"

"Of course."

I do, however, get out and walk her to her door. "Just making sure you're safe."

Ophelia slides her key into the lock, but before she turns the handle, she turns to me. "I think I'm scared of what may come tonight."

"I'll be beside you."

I pull her into a hug, and she rests her head against my chest. I wonder if she can feel the way my heart skips a few beats. I take notice of hers racing, but it could just be the fear of the nightmares.

I doubt it has anything to do with me.

As we pull away, my eyes catch hers. Our faces are not even six inches apart. It would only take a simple turn of the head.

But I won't take advantage of a moment like this. I pull back further and say, "Call me if you need to talk. And I'll call you when I get home."

I turn and walk back to my car, my heart aching to turn around again. I've never felt so sad to leave someone behind, even though it's temporary.

Is it temporary? Or was this day the start of something bigger?

Reconciling with my past isn't easy. My heart clenches every time I think about it. There's no greater heartbreak than losing someone the way I did. But there's also heartbreak in knowing that I should never have let things get this far.

I start to head back to the city, but on impulse I quickly turn my truck down the old dirt road leading to the gravesite. If I'm going to make peace, I have to do one more thing.

I shut my truck off on the dirt road, unable to make it any further. I get out, walking the worn paths to the different graves.

The cemetery isn't much. It's unkempt and forgotten, save for the few graves that are still cared for.

I find Moriah's headstone and take a seat across from it.

The grass brushes my hands and ankles. I hardly notice.

"You were right," I say softly. "You were always right. I shouldn't have doubted you."

Moriah was always conscious of the bond Ophelia and I had. She was scared of it, though I didn't realize it until later in our relationship. I was so focused on loving Moriah that I didn't see the things I should've.

"I'm falling for someone. I don't know if she will love me. I wish I had listened to you. Before everything happened the way it did."

I struggled to understand what was happening after the first argument we had. And every argument after that. I knew I didn't like Ophelia the way I loved Moriah.

But regardless of that, Moriah was worried about it. Until it reached a breaking point, one day when we were at the beach. I couldn't take it anymore. I had pushed Ophelia aside and Moriah didn't want me to let her back in, and I needed that to change. I wanted to leave, that day. Leave the relationship behind.

Moriah begged me to stay, but I didn't want to give her more chances to hurt me. And that decision to leave cost us everything.

It cost her life.

"There's something I can't deny," I tell her now. "Feelings I can't shake. And I want to prove to Ophelia that I'm sorry. But I don't know how."

I stay in the graveyard for a couple more minutes before I finally rise to my feet, brush off the seat of my jeans, and walk back to my car. I need to get back on the road to my apartment. It's time to get out of this town. At least for now.

23

Rook

"ROOK, YOU HAVE been given many chances to prove to us that you were working for the good of all Umbra. Do you deny that?"

I kneel before the Shadow Council. The only light in the room is shining on me. It impairs my vision, not that the shadows surrounding me are much to look at.

"I do not deny that I was given a chance at a new life as an Umbra. I also do not deny that I was given plenty of chances to prove I could keep up with the Way of the Shadow. And I am currently working on it."

A feminine shadow hisses from somewhere to my right. "'Working on it'? Is this all a game to you? We asked that you find souls to feed on, but you have been feeding off of the rations of souls that the other Umbra bring. You've not contributed anything further since the last time we spoke. We can't allow you to feed for free much longer. Tell us what you are planning."

I rise to my feet, hovering above the ground. "I am currently targeting four humans. I've had difficulty with one, as the fears inside her are deeply hidden. While I don't want to give up on her, I have turned my attention to the other three. But there's been a slight complication."

There's no complication. Everything is how I planned it. However, the Council has many elders who are not yet accepting of the way our powers could be used.

"I will deplete the life source of one for myself, then bring the life source of the others to help replenish what I have taken from the Hall of Umbra."

"Rook," the deep voice of the Council leader bellows. "That is not a plan. That is an ideal. What are you actively doing now?"

"I've trapped them in their nightmares, from which they will never wake up. As soon as they die in their sleep, I will take their life forces."

It seems so simple to say it this way, as if it were the easiest of tasks. I don't dare mention the deal I made with Atlas. He's not going to win this time, anyway. It's hardly a problem.

The Council whisper amongst themselves. Then one of the members sighs.

"You have one more chance to get this right, Rook. We don't take kindly to freeloaders. Have you not seen the punishments we have meted out to those who have committed lesser crimes than you?"

"Yes, Your Highest Ones."

"You have until the next official Council meeting to bring us the fruits of your labor. Otherwise, we will have to cut you off from our life sources, and you will fade into oblivion. Do you understand?"

"Yes." I bow my head.

"Meeting adjourned."

I'm cast back onto the roof of the city building I was resting on before the meeting was called.

My heart, or what remains of it , is heavy. I hate that I must do this—take broken hearts and nightmares, and feed off them.

It's far too painful to do. The human part of me remembers how it feels to be broken.

I want to be human again.

But there's no going back.

If I don't bring back life energy for the Hall of Shadows, I will soon be exiled. I will be cast into the oblivion, where I will soon fade from existence altogether. I don't have any room for error.

I can't fail.

24
Ophelia

THE BELL RINGS above the door of Darkest Night. A young mother and her small toddler come in, walking straight to the kids' section. I'm organizing a new shipment of board games by the checkout counter.

"Ophelia, are you feeling okay?"

I glance up at Priya, who's leaning over the counter.

"Yeah, why?"

"You just seem... distant. I'm not upset that you missed work yesterday. But it's not like you. And usually, I'd dismiss it, but you're acting..."

"Not like myself?" I supplement.

"Exactly."

I sigh. My reasons for being absent wouldn't make sense to her. They don't fully make sense to me yet. Obviously, I can't tell Priya that I'm disappointed I didn't get sent to a nightmare realm where I'd see Atlas.

I haven't even told her I'm reconnecting with Atlas at all, in the here and now, never mind in our dreams.

After all the history between me and Atlas, she'd be shocked, and probably worried, if I told her I was beginning to be friends with him again. But even though she knows none of this, I know she's worried for me.

"I'm okay. I just haven't been sleeping well lately." This isn't a lie. Sleep has been a struggle, and the only time I woke up feeling okay was when I found myself in Atlas's bed after almost dying in the ocean of his nightmares.

And that certainly isn't something I'm about to tell the only maternal figure in my life.

"If you need some time off, I could arrange it," Priya offers. "You work hard and I think you deserve it. Besides, I have more help around here."

I follow Priya's glance over to her formerly estranged husband, Matthew. When I saw him come in earlier, I didn't know how to greet him. It's a bit unsettling to have him here again after so long. He's much taller than I remember him being; his hair is still that dusty shade of blond. He's stocking books in the young adult section, whistling a tune I don't recognize.

Priya seems happy about his return. And as far as I can tell, he's been really helpful around the bookstore.

Regardless, taking time off isn't something I generally do. I'm always wanting to work to keep distracted.

My instinct is to say no, to insist I can work and make it happen. But right now, some time off sounds almost blissful. Maybe I could visit Atlas. Or at least relax a little.

"I might take you up on that," I say, relenting. "It might be nice to take a break."

Priya smiles. "You have been working very hard, and I think the rest would do you some good. I know whatever is bothering you, you'll figure it out. And just know you can come to me when you feel safe."

Safe.

It's a feeling I've chased for most of my life, but I never truly felt it until I was in Atlas's arms the other day. He felt like home.

So much change in such a small amount of time. If anyone could understand that feeling, it's Priya. But I'm not ready to talk about it.

"Maybe I could take the next couple of days?"

"Of course. Take tomorrow and the weekend. You can come back on Tuesday. That will give me time to really observe Matthew. See if he's serious about working here again."

That seems fair enough to me. A few days of rest couldn't hurt.

I finish my shift without much happening. Outside, as I leave the store, I inhale the soft autumn air. I can't shake the feeling that someone is watching me. I look around, but there's nothing. I sense it must be Rook. I wonder if he's invisible in the daylight. Or maybe he's only able to communicate through dreams.

I glance over at Every Brew, where Reya is finishing up her shift. I need to talk to someone about what's going on. I don't know if Reya will believe me or even understand. But I need to feel less alone.

I enter the café, Reya's back turned to me. "Sorry, we're closed for the night."

"I don't want coffee."

Reya turns around, a small smile forming on her face. "Oh, Ophelia. I'm surprised to see you."

"I need some help."

Reya walks over to the doors, locking them. She's the assistant manager, so it's her night to close. "I sent everyone home. It was a slow night, so I'm just closing by myself," she explains.

She motions for me to have a seat at the bar, so I do. "Your usual?"

"Yes, please."

She gets to work on a hot chocolate with extra whip cream. She sets two steaming mugs down, one for herself and one for me.

"All right. Spill."

I think of all the ways I could try to explain what's been going on in my life right now. But I'm worried that it won't seem real.

So I start with the easier, more believable part of the story. "I've started talking to Atlas again."

"Is there a reason? Did you run into each other while he was in town?"

I shake my head. "I know what I'm going to tell you is going to seem crazy, but I need someone to talk to about this. And you've been by my side for so long. I know you'll listen to me."

Taking a deep breath, I tell her everything. I tell her about the dreams, the butterflies, and Rook. I leave out the more intimate details of Atlas's nightmare. I also don't tell her I woke up in his bed. Something about that moment feels private, between me and Atlas.

Reya takes in every word I say, her eyes crinkling

at the edges as she listens. I can't tell whether she thinks I'm crazy or if she believes what I'm saying.

When I finish, the coffee shop is quieter than it was when I walked in. I hold my mug of hot chocolate; all warmth having fled from my body.

Reya stands up straight and says, "I believe you."

"Really?"

"I believe you because I know about the Shadow Realm. I know about Umbra. I never thought one would find itself here. They don't usually haunt places like this."

"Wait, you know about the creature that's haunting me and Atlas?"

"Yes. I can't really talk about why right now. But I hope you'll trust me."

I trust her more than ever now. "So how do we get rid of him?"

Reya sighs. "Well, you made a deal. Umbra are big on promises and deals. Unfortunately, you'll have to see it through. And hopefully you'll come out on top."

"So if they don't usually haunt places like this, where do they go?"

Reya begins to walk back and forth behind the coffee bar. "Umbra crave specific energy. That energy is usually found in places with high activity. That's not to say small towns are all safe, or big cities have a high population of Umbra. It's just about the energy a place has. And we've never had that here, for as long as I've lived her, anyway. But there's a first time for everything."

I wonder what it means for Rook to be here. I wonder what made him choose me. Or what made him choose Atlas.

The sun has long since set. Reya finishes cleaning and then we walk home together. We don't talk much, walking in comfortable silence. My mind is reeling with all the things Reya knows, with her understanding of what I'm going through.

When we stop at the corner that separates my street from hers, she puts a hand on my shoulder. "Whatever you do, don't make any more deals with him. The Umbra. Stay strong. And if you get sucked into a dream, do whatever it takes to get out. Because you don't want to become one of them."

WHEN I GET home, I lock the doors, check the locks on the windows, and keep the curtains drawn shut. Yet the feeling that something is watching me never goes away.

I suppose a shadow figure isn't kept away by simple locks and doors. He did manage to enter my head when my house was locked tight.

I rest on the couch for a few minutes; figuring out what to make for dinner is up to me. Dad won't be home for a few more hours. Sometimes I wish he was home more. I'd feel safer in times like this. But trying to explain to him what's going on would be nearly impossible. Besides, his work is his method of coping.

Every noise startles me. I'm constantly checking over my shoulder, inspecting every shadow that moves in the house.

The unsettled feeling doesn't leave. I consider calling Atlas, but I decide against it. Whoever is out there, I have a feeling I will meet them soon, in my dreams.

25

Ophelia

Sixteen Years Old

I SEE ATLAS and Moriah at lunch. Not that I sit with them. But I see them across the room, watching something on Moriah's phone. Laughing. Leaning their heads together.

I look away, unable to take the strain it puts on my heart.

I haven't spoken to Atlas in days. He hasn't tried to call or text me, either. I don't need to hear from him every day, but this isn't usually us.

It's gotten worse the longer he's been dating Moriah.

After the dance two years ago, they started hanging out more without me. I knew what it meant. I knew I'd lost him.

And honestly, I've coped with that. I've been able to accept that he didn't have feelings for me. But

Moriah grew colder towards me, trying to keep me at a distance. I didn't understand then, and I still don't understand, when she's the one who was hurting me all along.

Atlas still hangs out with me when he can, or talks to me in the hallway. But for the past few days, I've not heard anything.

Not even his usual goodnight texts.

I take a bite of my sandwich, trying to keep my attention away from everything I'm losing.

Even if he isn't mine, I love him. All I want is to have my best friend back.

"Is this seat taken?"

I look up to see Milo Pierce. We share a couple of classes, but other than that, I've never really spoken to him. His chestnut hair falls a little into his eyes, which are a warm brown. He's dressed in all dark clothes, which lends to his reputation.

I watch him carefully. "No, go ahead."

Everyone refers to him as a troublemaker or rebellious. I've never paid enough attention to him to really know anything about his reputation, other than hearing the whispers in the hallway. He's somewhat of an outcast, despite many of the girls having secret crushes on him. Some say he deals drugs. Some say he's done time in prison. I don't like rumors, so I never listen.

He sits across from me, setting his lunch down. "I've noticed you've been sitting alone for the better part of the month," he says. "Not that it's any of my business, but people know you've been cast aside since your two best friends started dating each other." He jerks his chin over to where Moriah and Atlas are sitting.

I shrug. "That's life, isn't it?"

"It doesn't have to be." He sighs. "I'm amazed you didn't try to stop it."

I lean back. "No offense, Milo, but I don't really know you. So how is it you know all these things about me?"

He doesn't seem offended or even bothered by this question. "I happen to notice when other loners pass through the halls. People here avoid me because most of them took one look at me when I moved into town, heard a twisted story about my past, and decided I'm not someone to get to know. But you... you were never a loner until those two started getting closer. Now I've seen you striking out on your own."

He takes a spoonful of what appears to be soup he brought from home.

"Honestly, it's a little jarring for you to be observing me this much," I tell him.

He shrugs. "I observe everyone. I have time to watch things when no one talks to me."

"And so you decided you wanted to talk to me in person and see if all your theories are correct?"

"No. You looked lonely and I thought it might be nice to keep you company. Because I know what it feels like to be pushed out of your friend group when two of the friends start getting romantically involved."

I frown. "Well... thank you. I'm sorry if I came off harsh. I'm just... frustrated."

"You're also in love with Atlas Jameson."

I nearly choke on my sandwich. "What?"

Milo laughs, and the sound is surprisingly warm, one that invites me to laugh with him. Except I'm too busy being embarrassed to join him in the revelry.

He leans back in his seat. "That one was made up, but based on your reaction, I can assume I struck a nerve."

"No. That's not it. Atlas has been my best friend since we were young. The idea that I would be in love with him is strange."

I can try to cover it up, right? Milo doesn't know everything. I can gain the upper hand here.

He crosses his arms. "Look, if you haven't noticed, I don't have friends. Your secret's safe with me. I won't bring it up again unless you want it brought up."

"No."

"Isn't this weather quite nice?" He grins and then takes another spoonful of soup.

Milo is a mystery. A sixteen-year-old guy who can see through everyone's deepest thoughts and secrets, who comes to join lonely people for lunch just because they look sad. Yet he'll switch topics the moment things start getting uncomfortable for the other person. What is his game?

I lean forward, resting my elbows on the table. "Since you're seeing through everything, I want to ask something."

"What's that?"

"Why do you have a reputation for being a bad guy?"

He laughs. "Is that what my reputation is?"

"I have a hard time believing you don't know, considering you seem to know everything about everyone else. You must be self-aware."

He smirks, and it's almost cute. Almost. "How observant. Well, truthfully, the reputation came from my old school. I stood up for a kid who was being bullied. But the principal's niece was there and because I had turned her down for the dance, she decided to embellish the story so I'd get in trouble. But then something else happened."

"And that something was?"

"I might've been arrested for getting into a fight with the bully the next day when I saw him doing something else that was just as bad. Things got pretty physical, and even though he started it, they saw me as the person who instigated the whole thing because I was the one who threw the first punch."

"You don't seem like the type to fight," I say. Because he doesn't. He's far too logical for that. At least, that's how he seems.

"I'm not usually. But the guy was screaming at his girlfriend in the hallway and I went up and told him to cut it out. He swung the first couple of times. I fought back to defend myself. Except he ended up with a broken nose because when he went to hit me, he tripped and fell face first into the lockers. He was fine, but his parents would not stop fighting to get me out of school. The police agreed it was self-defense after watching the footage, but by that point, the story had gotten twisted."

He grimaces, as if this is painful for him to talk about. I had heard the whispers in the girls' bathroom or in the hallway about him beating someone up. But I never knew how much truth there was to the rumors.

"I only fight to protect the innocent," he says. "But you don't have to worry. My fighting days are over."

The story is jarring, but not many people are so candid about being arrested. Milo doesn't seem bothered by this detail of his past. He eats his soup, unperturbed that he's told me the real reason behind his reputation. Maybe it's because it was so long ago. I admire that he doesn't let his past define his present.

At this moment, I realize that I don't feel as lonely as I did before he sat here. For a change, I'm not thinking about Atlas and Moriah. I glance over one more time. They're lost in conversation, heads bent close. No care for the world around them.

I look back to Milo. "I'm sorry I judged you without knowing you," I say.

He shrugs, but a small smile plays on his lips. "I'm used to people making up their minds about me, but I'm not used to being apologized to, so that's refreshing."

For the next while, we eat our lunches and chat. Milo listens to me go on and on about my interests and I listen to his. It's easy, and we almost get too caught up in conversation to remember to get to class.

When we both rise from the table, I catch Atlas's eye. He looks concerned. I look away.

I'm not going to explain myself to him.

He left me to my own devices. I'm allowed to make new friends.

26

Atlas

The rain pours heavily outside the cave.

The cave?

I glance around. Ophelia is lying on the cave floor. She hasn't woken up in the dream yet.

But we're not alone. Embarrassingly, something about that disappoints me.

Carter, my roommate, stands at the mouth of the cave, looking out into the world beyond.

I run a hand through my hair, unsure if he even knows we're here.

This must not be Ophelia's fear to overcome yet. Only Rook—the Mastermind—would know why Carter is even here.

Ophelia starts to awaken, confused and dazed. "I thought you went home," she mumbles sleepily.

"We're in a dream. And it's not either of ours."

This catches her attention. She rises to her feet beside me. "Who's that?"

"My roommate. But I don't know if he's aware we're here or if we have to save him without him knowing anything."

"I thought I just had to face my fear and then we'd be free."

"Yeah, well, apparently Rook put us on a side quest."

Ophelia nods slowly, but glances over at Carter.

He doesn't seem to be aware of us, so I make the first move to approach him. He stares out into the forest below the cave. Lots of evergreen trees as far as the eye can see. For a moment, I'm caught up in the beauty of nature. Living in a city for so long makes me crave something like this.

"Carter," I begin.

"I wonder what the game is," he says. "You being here in my dreams, too. What fear he's making me face."

"Who?"

"The Mastermind," he says with fear lacing his tone.

"You know the Mastermind?" Ophelia says from behind us.

Carter turns, facing her. "Yes. He came to me in a dream one night and declared himself a Soul Eater. I have to fight through a series of trials in order to keep my soul. Twisted, isn't it? I thought at first it was a terrible nightmare concocted by my imagination since I have an active one. But then things started occurring in my waking life that can't be explained by anything other than some strange being like the Mastermind."

Ophelia looks at me, slightly dazed. "The Mastermind?"

I tilt my head and look back at Carter. "You mean Rook?"

Carter shrugs. "The Umbra. He didn't introduce himself as anything other than the Mastermind. He's spoken more to you?"

"He's talked too much," I say, rolling my eyes.

Carter studies Ophelia for a moment. "You… you're Atlas's childhood friend he can't get over, right?"

Oh, great. Airing my secrets.

"I'm Ophelia." She sticks her hand out for him to shake. He takes it. She doesn't respond to his comment about me, which I'm grateful for.

"Atlas left out how beautiful you are in all his stories."

She blushes.

Time for a change of subject. "Okay, so what exactly are we supposed to do?"

Carter sighs, looking out into the rain again. "The way I understand it, we have to face our fears. I assume this must have something to do with mine."

I cross my arms, leaning my back against the cave wall. "I already faced mine."

Carter looks back at us. Ophelia exchanges a look with me. She's seeking a silent answer to a question between us: Do we tell Carter?

I push off from the wall and go over to stand beside her, then turn back to Carter. "I want to know that this is the real Carter," I tell him. "This could be another scam made up by the Mastermind."

Carter nods. "Fair enough."

"Tell me something only the real Carter would know."

Carter smirked. "You sure you want me to do that?"

I glance at Ophelia.

"Could be a trap," she says quietly. "Maybe he's not real and doesn't know something that only you two would know."

I look back to Carter, my arms crossed against my chest. "Go ahead."

Carter's smirk turns into a devilish smile. "I met my girlfriend at a party where she was actually making out with you."

The heat that surges through my entire body burns me from the inside out. "You had so many things you could've said and you went with that?"

Only Carter, Rebecca, and I know that story. And there's more to it than that. But I glance at Ophelia, who's trying not to laugh.

"I'd like to hear that story someday," she quips.

Carter smiles widely. "When Atlas brings you around, I'll tell you."

"Okay." I step between them. "Enough of that story. Let's get on with this. Obviously, we have to help you face your fear. So, what's the plot of your nightmare? Do you know anything yet?"

Carter smiles, but a bitter look taints his eyes. "I've been trapped in this recurring nightmare every time I go to sleep because at the end, I die every time. I know this dream inside and out. And this dream is a combination of moments in my life. The cave, for when I went exploring in Europe. The forest, for when I went backpacking through the forests of the east coast."

I nod, taking a seat on a large rock. "The rain isn't letting up. Are we supposed to wait it out?"

"No. It won't stop raining here."

Ophelia runs a hand through her hair. "How do you know?"

"Because it rained the day that my step-sister died."

27

Atlas

Seventeen Years Old

FRIDAY NIGHTS ARE usually date nights for Moriah and me. It's an easy night; usually, we head to a burger joint a few towns over.

Moriah laces her fingers through mine as we walk through the parking lot.

"I wish you'd worn your button-down shirt," she says, sighing.

"It's not a fancy place. Besides, I didn't know you wanted to dress up."

"Date night is always a reason to dress up. But it's not a big deal."

The way she says it doesn't convince me that it's not actually a big deal. But I don't push the subject further. I don't care if Moriah wants us to dress up for our dates, but I would appreciate more communication.

I'm not dressed badly. I'm in a dark blue band tee and jeans. Moriah is wearing a simple dress that's not super fancy. I don't see the big deal.

We find a booth near the window and a waitress takes our order.

Moriah sits across from me, texting one of her friends while we wait for the food.

I don't really mind, though.

My phone chimes and I see a text from Ophelia.

I decide to respond since Moriah is also on her phone.

Ophelia: hey are you busy?

Me: I'm a few towns over getting burgers with Moriah. Shouldn't be late getting back tho. Why?

Ophelia: nevermind. new book came out. thought we could go check it out at the bookstore.

Me: wanna go tomorrow?

Ophelia: sounds good :)

It's been a while since I've gone to the bookstore with Ophelia. Or even gotten to hang out with her.

"Who was that?" Moriah asks, her voice a bit cold.

"Why?"

"You're smiling, and you never smile like that when you text."

I shrug. "It's just Ophelia."

Moriah sets her phone down. "We're on a date right now, though."

"You were on your phone, too."

Moriah frowns. "Only for a moment. I was responding to a text. You were texting for a little bit. I want us to focus on each other."

"We've been dating for over a year, Moriah. I think it's okay for me to text my best friend while we wait for our dinner to arrive."

Before Moriah can respond, the waitress returns with two burger combos. I thank her as she bounces away.

"Okay, let's make a deal," I say. "I won't get on my phone while we eat, but that means you can't either."

Moriah's frown deepens and I know she's frustrated. I don't understand why she seems to want to control my time talking to other people. Especially when I'm talking to Ophelia.

There's something more to the frustration than just me using my phone. Whatever it is, I don't like it.

But maybe it's been a stressful week; maybe she's just tired and lashing out. I don't press it further. It's not worth it.

28

I SPEND MY nights in the air when my targets are dreaming. I can't interfere too much with the nightmares. Not when I've had them set in motion already. I can visit them, observe them, but I don't want to interfere.

I land on the roof of an apartment building, taking in the view of the city at night.

But the pleasure fades quickly: I agreed to meet one of the Shadow Wielders here. Shadow Wielders are high-ranking officers of the Shadow Realm. They often are tasked with guarding the Council. They also have access to a lot of information.

I want to know how to return to human form. There has to be a way to do it.

"Rook," says a voice behind me. "Come closer to the shadows."

I turn away from the city lights and walk towards Trig, the Shadow Wielder.

"You wanted to see me, Rook? What was so important that you would wish me to burn energy to meet here in the mortal realm?"

"I'm in a bit of trouble in the Shadow Realm."

Trig laughs. If he had eyes, they'd probably water. When he collects himself, he shakes his head. "You think I don't know that? I've heard of your escapades and your lack of production. I'd hate to see you be exiled into the outer world. There's no coming back from places like that. And unlike the Council, I like you."

I grip his shoulders. "That's why I need your help. I need to know how to return to human form."

Trig stiffens, if that's even possible for a Shadow Wielder, and floats away, out of my reach. "You want to return to human life? You know you're not supposed to feel tethered to your human life."

"I know. But here I am. So how do I do this?"

Trig sighs. "You can beg the Shadow Council, but they'll want to make a bargain with you. They'll want to see you do enough work to supply the loss you will be creating. Although, since it's you we're talking about, that's not a heavy loss." He pauses, letting that sink in. "There is one other way, a back door to the Shadow Curse. But I don't know what kind of trouble I can get into if I tell you."

"I won't breathe a word to another shadow soul."

Trig looks around, then lowers his voice. "Find someone human to fall in love with you. If you can get that to happen, you'll break the curse."

I stare at the ground. *Someone human would never love a creature like me.*

Trig is gone before I can ask any more questions, leaving me in the dark.

Finding someone to love me in this form? It's almost impossible. But there is one girl from my past life who believed in things that were supposedly beyond the impossible. Someone I never got over. And maybe it's time I fix that.

29

Ophelia

I'M SPEECHLESS.

All this time...

"You're Moriah's step-brother."

Carter's face is grim. I study him for any sign that he's lying. But he doesn't show anything other than pure grief and anguish.

"You lived with your mom. Your dad married Moriah's mom. You felt betrayed by your father. You wanted nothing to do with anyone."

"Partially true. I did meet Moriah, and we were both angsty teenagers, angry that our parents let this happen. We formed a solid bond. We became friends. We texted all the time. And obviously, she spoke of me to you since you knew all of that."

"I didn't know you were Atlas's roommate, though." I look between them.

Atlas shrugs. "I didn't know it was relevant since

you hadn't met Carter yet, and we're… trying to figure out where we stand in general."

Carter nods. "Fair enough. I wasn't home from work when you were in the city, either. It really wouldn't have come up that day. And as far as I can tell, that's the only day you two have been friendly again."

"It is. After Atlas faced his fear, we woke up in his bed."

Carter smirks at Atlas, eyes alight with excitement. "Now *that* was a detail left out of the conversation we had."

"A detail that wasn't supposed to be revealed," Atlas says, glancing at me, eyes full of sorrow at my betrayal.

I smile coolly at him. "Well, we can't hide our secrets from your roommate, now, can we? Besides, that didn't happen on purpose. It was only because… well, I can't give away the contents of the dream yet, but it makes sense."

Carter shakes his head, amused, as he turns to face the wall of rain again. "I can't wait to dive into that juicy story, but if we want to get out of this alive, we need to venture beyond this cave. I know exactly where we're going. I've never made it beyond this dream before. I wake up, and then it starts over again the next night. I need help. And I think you two might be the key to escaping my nightmare."

"What do we need to do?" I ask him.

He turns back to face us. "We're venturing into a graveyard to obtain a magical amulet. That isn't the fearful part, though. It's only the plot of the story that has to unfold to force me to face the thing I fear most."

The way he speaks is so poetic, every word making

this seem like a fairy tale come to life, a fantastical story from one of the books that line Priya's shelves.

"In the rain?"

"In the rain. I've hated rainy days since Moriah died. But I think that is only one layer of the story, just one of the things I have to face. Because every time I've done this before it's rained, and that has not changed."

"So we can rule out rain being the fear." Atlas confirms my thoughts out loud.

"If rain isn't the fear, and the journey to the amulet isn't the fear, then what is?"

Carter's face becomes grim once again. "The thing I fear most? That would be death."

30

Ophelia

Sixteen Years Old

I STARE AT the text on my phone, tears building in my eyes. I glance around the park, making sure no one notices me.

Atlas: sorry I can't make it... Moriah's step-brother is in town and she wants me to meet him. Meet up tomorrow?

I don't give him the dignity of a response. Instead, I let my phone rest on my lap, pretending he didn't just stab a knife into my heart once again.

"Ophelia?"

I open my eyes, finding Milo standing in front of me in running shorts and a tank top. He's pulled one earbud out of his ear to talk to me.

I quickly wipe my eyes. "Hey, Milo."

"Are you okay?"

I could make up some lie, tell him everything is great. He could continue on his run. I could continue sitting in misery alone, then eventually go home and be mad about the number of times Atlas has ditched me for Moriah.

"I was supposed to meet Atlas here," I say instead. Something about Milo's kind eyes makes me want to say the truth, even if I don't really want to face it.

"I'm guessing he's not coming?"

I shake my head. "Something came up again."

"With his girlfriend." He doesn't say it like a question because we both know it isn't one.

"Yeah. But honestly, it's fine. I have so much to do today. I should probably head home."

"Or... you could walk the track with me. I'm not really in the mood to run today. A nice walk always clears my head."

I rise from the bench, slipping my phone into my back pocket without another thought. "I would love to walk." I smile.

Milo takes out his earbuds, stuffing them in his pocket. "I take it Atlas abandons his plans with you a lot."

Another question that isn't a question because the answer is clear.

"Yeah, he does. I think what hurts me the most about it is that Atlas and I have been best friends since we were really young. And he promised me that we wouldn't change just because he was dating Moriah. We were all friends for a while, and at first, I hung out with Moriah a bit, just the two of us. But now Moriah doesn't really talk to me unless it's all three of us. And Atlas... well, he's always busy."

"What will he do when they break up?"

"They will probably never break up. They're perfect for each other." I let the bitterness slip into my voice, hoping Milo doesn't notice.

"You liked Atlas before she did."

Of course he notices. "I don't know. All I know is I miss my best friend."

"You do know. You liked him as more than a friend. Maybe not now. But you did before all of this."

I cross my arms defensively. "I guess I did. But it doesn't matter. That's not what's important to me. What's important is that he's at least in my life."

Milo shrugs. "Look, I know you think they'll be together forever, but Moriah is not good for him. I know it's weird for me to say that. I don't know either of them well enough. But I have noticed she's very controlling. Eventually, their castle will crumble and he'll come to you to pick up the pieces. The question you have to ask yourself is... will it be too late?"

I'm silent for a moment, wondering if it's true. Every time I'm third-wheeling, they seem perfect. But Milo is someone who observes more than the average person. Even if what he says is true, there is the question of whether I'll be here for Atlas.

"I don't think that's much of a question," I finally say. "Of course I'll be here. He's not intentionally hurting me. He thinks it's okay. He doesn't realize what he's doing, and even though it's terrible and I should let him figure it out, if they were to break up, I would be here to help him. If he needed me to be, that is."

"You're pretty generous to let him ignore you."

"He doesn't know he's ignoring me. He answers all

my texts. If I call about a homework question, he answers right away. He drives me home from school. It doesn't register in his mind that he's blowing me off. And I will probably talk to him about it once I'm no longer angry."

Milo smiles. "I'm glad you're mature about it."

"I don't want to be. But I'm practically raising myself, so I have to be an adult about this."

Milo doesn't question what I mean, just nods as though he understands. Maybe he does.

"Enough about me. What about you?"

He smiles. "What do you want to know?"

"I don't know. What do you want to reveal?"

He pauses for a moment, as though he's considering his next words. "My parents don't really support my dreams. I'm working on getting two jobs so I can support myself the minute I turn eighteen."

"What are your dreams?"

"I want to study art in college. They want me to follow the family business... which I definitely don't want to talk about."

I nod. "Fair enough. You like to draw, right? I've seen you drawing sometimes at school."

"Yeah, but it's more than that. I want to know the history of all the greatest art in the world. I want to paint and draw and have my pieces shown in museums and galleries, but I also want to know about all the other art that exists in the world."

Dreams like this seem simple, yet perfect. And the way he talks about his ambitions makes him seem like he's already got his life figured out. Me, not so much. I don't see myself going to college after high school. I love learning, but I don't have a clue what I'd want to learn. Besides that, I need to get a job instead, start saving up.

"I like your dreams."

Milo smiles as though this is the best thing he's heard.

I like his smile, too. But I don't say that out loud. I don't know if I'm ready for the tangle of feelings that are developing beneath the surface. Am I really over Atlas? Would it even be fair to start having feelings for someone else?

In this moment, though, I throw all of that to the side, taking in the time with Milo.

If it takes a little support to make him happy, then I'll support him.

He deserves a little bit of happiness.

31

Atlas

I NO LONGER notice I'm soaked because I've long since gone numb to the cold rain that coats every inch of my body. Ophelia shivers as she walks next to me.

Carter is a few dozen feet ahead of us, leading the way through this mysterious forest. Suddenly, he turns and begins running back to us, whisper-yelling that he's found something.

He runs off again in the direction of whatever it is he's found. I stay behind and walk with Ophelia. I would offer her my arm, but I'm not any warmer than she is.

Up ahead, there are scattered gravestones shrouded in mist. The rain is also lighter now. Once we get closer to the actual graveyard, the rain dissipates completely, becoming a thick, humid fog.

Much like the fog that shrouded the graveyard the day Moriah was buried.

"At least it's warmer here," I say softly to Ophelia.
She nods, still shivering.

Carter is studying each grave marker, looking for whatever it is we're supposed to find.

"What are we supposed to keep an eye out for?"

"The beasts."

"The *what*?"

Carter glances up. "I've come close to finding the amulet before. Each time I get close, though, there's some horrific monster that comes to fight me. I lose. I wake up. And then, the next night when I fall asleep, I end up back here. But this time, it'll be different. This time, you'll be here to warn me of the beast."

Ophelia glances at me, then at Carter. "W-what do you m-mean, you lose?"

"I run away. I wake myself up before it can kill me."

I pace back and forth, trying to generate body heat. I'm soaked to the bone and my clothes aren't helping matters much. I peel my shirt off, laying it on one of the gravestones to dry. Ophelia's eyes widen and she quickly looks away from me. There's a flush on her cheeks, and I want to pull her closer, ask her why she's blushing. But I have work to do.

Carter continues searching every stone, though I can tell he's done this a number of times.

There's a roar in the distance, startling all of us. Carter pales at the sound. "That's the beast. We have to get out of here. Back to the cave."

He takes off, sprinting. Ophelia goes after him. I grab my shirt and run, back into the cold rain. It hits my bare back and chest like ice.

I try to keep a close eye on Ophelia, my vision

blurring in the rain. We hear the roar again, closer this time. Ophelia trips and falls onto the muddy earth. She says something about her ankle that I barely register. Instinct kicks in and I pick her up and carry her the rest of the way, bridal style.

Once in the cave, we both collapse to the ground.

Carter is there already. He frowns, staring out the cave door into the open. "I have turned over every gravestone in that place. I know that graveyard like the back of my hand at this point. Yet I've not found the amulet."

"We almost died out there," I say roughly, catching my breath. "Maybe give us a second before you start your pity party."

"A-atlas." Ophelia's voice shakes with her body. "I-it's okay."

Carter looks absolutely grim when he sees the condition Ophelia is in.

"I shouldn't have made you come."

Ophelia shudders as she sits up against the cave wall. "Rook m-made us. N-not you."

Carter closes his eyes for a moment. Then a fire appears in the center of the cave.

I glance between the orange flames and him. "How did you do that?"

"It's my dream. I can manipulate it slightly to provide for me. I just can't change the bigger picture of it. We need warmth, so I thought of a nice fire. And some blankets. You two need to get out of your wet clothes. You can wrap yourselves in the blankets while your clothes dry."

Carter and I turn away, letting Ophelia strip down

first. She wraps herself in a huge blanket and sits by the fire while her shirt and pants dry.

She closes her eyes when I go to take my pants off. I wrap another blanket around my shoulders and sit next to her. "It will warm us up faster if we get closer."

Carter shakes his head and rolls his eyes at me. "You have no game when it comes to women."

Ophelia blushes.

I quickly defend myself. "I don't mean like that. I'm trying to prevent us from dying."

Ophelia rests her head on my shoulder. "I know." She then turns her attention to my roommate. "Are you going to use the third blanket?"

He shakes his head. "The rain doesn't affect me like it did you two. Don't worry about me. We'll probably wake up soon, anyway."

Ophelia sighs softly, though I feel it more than hear it. Then she sits bolt upright. "Wait a second... Carter, before we left this cave, what did you say your fear was?"

"Death."

"Do you ever fight the beast, or do you retreat each time?"

"I wouldn't call it retreating to have a desire for self-preservation."

"He retreats," I say, not unkindly. I get it.

"Atlas feared the ocean and drowning," says Ophelia. "But when I fell off the ship in his nightmare, he dove in headfirst to save me. You have to face the beast, Carter. You have to die."

Everything she's saying makes sense, but I can tell it's all lost on Carter.

"I'm not ready to die. I have so much more to live for."

"You won't really die. This is a dream."

"How do you know? How do you know the beast won't kill me for real and I'll just die in my sleep?"

Ophelia smiles. "Because if you die, the Soul Eater won't have a soul to feast on. I didn't drown. I didn't wake up soaked in water. Atlas didn't either. The only time something came from our shared dream was—"

I elbow Ophelia and she stops, immediately understanding.

Carter doesn't seem to notice. He begins pacing back and forth in front of the mouth of the cave. "It sounds risky."

Ophelia leans her head on my shoulder again. "Sometimes you have to take risks to survive."

32

Atlas

Seventeen Years Old

MORIAH'S HAND IS locked in mine. We're walking towards the exit of the Autumn Festival. We've been here for a couple of hours. We've ridden some of the rides, played a lot of the games, and eaten more fair food than anyone should ever ingest in a lifetime.

That's when I see Ophelia.

And Milo.

Every time I see her with Milo, something in me grows a bit angrier. He's got a bad reputation and a worse attitude about it. He doesn't care what people think. I think he's just careless about all of it. But she's been hanging around him a lot.

I see him take her hand and spin her gently. Words are exchanged—and then she kisses him. I freeze. Beside me, Moriah stops walking and looks up at me.

She follows my gaze, seeing Milo as he kisses Ophelia again.

"Oh, wow. Good for her. I'm glad she's finally moving on."

"Moving on?"

Moriah shrugs. "She had a crush on you back when we were all friends."

That... is news to me.

"Aren't we all still friends?" I ask her, genuinely puzzled.

Moriah runs her free hand through her hair as we continue to walk to the exit. "I don't know. Ophelia hasn't wanted to talk to me lately. I think she's mad I'm the one dating you."

I watch Ophelia and Milo as they run towards the food stands. But I don't watch long.

If he's kind to her, that's all that matters.

How did I not know my best friend liked me as more than a friend?

Moriah leans against my arm. "Besides, she's clearly moved on. When was the last time you actually hung out with her?"

"Well... there were many times we were supposed to, but it always fell through." Because of me. Because I put Moriah first.

I'm starting to realize that may have been the wrong thing to do. Ophelia stopped reaching out to me. And it's my fault.

Moriah sighs. "Sometimes people fade into the background of our lives. And maybe we've faded out of Ophelia's life. Her attention is on Milo now. Best if we just let it be. She'll come back if she wants to."

Something doesn't sit right about any of that, but I don't say anything about it.

I DRIVE MORIAH home from the festival. I pull up in front of her house, and she leans over the armrest and places her hand on my face, turning me to look at her. Her lips find mine in a slow, gentle kiss. She pulls away, smiling. "I had a great time tonight. Thanks for taking me."

"Of course. I'll see you later?"

"Always, baby. Always."

She gets out of my truck and I wait until she's safely inside to pull away.

My mind is on Ophelia.

And my heart is full of regret.

Something inside of me is torn between listening to Moriah's words and paying attention to my own feelings. *Maybe I should reach out to Ophelia...*

When I pull up in front of my house, I decide that it's my fault Ophelia's pulled away from us. If she really did like me, and she really was hurt that I chose Moriah, I need to make things right. I pull out my phone.

Me: hey do you think we can talk soon?

Ophelia: about what?

Me: I've been a crappy friend

Ophelia: I can't argue there. When do you want to talk?

Me: tomorrow?

Ophelia: okay. Text me in the morning and I'll let you know if I'm free

Me: okay. See you then

33

Ophelia

DARKNESS FALLS, AND it's pitch black now inside the cave. The fire has long since burned out, but a new problem exists. There's a growling nearby. The beast may have followed us, or perhaps there are more monsters lying in wait.

Now it's just about waiting for the daylight to return.

Carter stopped pacing a while ago. Now, he's sitting on the ground, looking out into the endless forest.

From here, it's easy to see the graveyard. No beast lurks, at least not that I can see. But we can hear it growling.

It's probably hiding in the trees.

Atlas sleeps, wrapped up in the blanket. I've changed back into my damp clothes, not wanting to stay half-undressed forever.

"You know you'll wake up immediately, and then everything will be okay," I say to Carter, keeping my voice low to as not to wake Atlas.

Carter shakes his head. "I don't know that. What if this is a twisted plot to allow the beast to eat my soul? There are so many things this could be."

"You have to face your fear. It's the only way out of this place."

"I've usually woken up by now. I guess because we're all here now, I can't get out of my fate."

He rises to his feet, glancing back at Atlas. "I'm going now."

My heart stops. "What?"

"Whatever happens, you both don't need to see it. I will go. You'll know I succeeded when we all wake up." He starts towards the mouth of the cave, but pauses just before the curtain of rain. "And in the event I do die for real... tell Atlas he still can't have my PlayStation."

I roll my eyes, but nod firmly. "You're not going to die for real. This is a simulation. But I don't think you should go it alone."

Carter shakes his head. "I don't think anyone should see how this goes down. It's better this way."

Before I can protest further, he's outside, in the darkness. I get to my feet and pace, unsure if I should wake Atlas up to help me follow Carter, or if we should respect his wishes.

Time seems to tick by slowly, painfully.

After a while, Atlas wakes up, rubbing his eyes. "Sleeping inside a dream is weird." He glances around. "Where's Carter?"

"He..."

I don't have to finish before Atlas has shot up, his blanket falling off him. I catch a glimpse of his boxers. My eyes widen with embarrassment and I quickly turn away. I hate that I also noticed his six-pack. "Maybe put your clothes on?" I suggest.

"Sorry," he says, grabbing his shirt and pants. "Why did he go alone?" He turns away from me and dresses quickly.

"He said he didn't want us to see what happens."

"Well, you know we're going to have to go and hunt him down, right?"

I sigh. "Shouldn't we respect his wishes?"

He puts a hand on my shoulder, gently turning me to face him. "If I'd respected *your* wishes about leaving you alone, you would've drowned."

I cut my eyes at him. "That was a very different situation."

"Life or death. Sounds similar to this one, too."

"He has to face his fear for us to get out of here."

Atlas frowns. "I'm going to track him down. I won't let him do this alone. If you don't feel safe going, I completely understand, and I'll support your decision to wait in the cave. But I can't let him do this."

Atlas's eyes are stormy with passion and fear—Carter's wishes be damned.

"Okay," I say. "I'll come with you."

The rainy forest at night is not easy to navigate, but I follow Atlas's lead.

We find ourselves in the graveyard, hiding behind trees so Carter doesn't see us.

He's perched on a gravestone, looking peaceful. His eyes are closed, and his mouth is saying words, but we can't hear them over the rain. I notice immediately he's clutching the amulet he's spent every dream looking for. It glows in the muted light, brighter than anything I've ever seen.

Soon, a deafening roar fills the air, and something large and furry comes stumbling into the graveyard. Carter rises, turning to face the creature that has come to take his life.

"Come get me," he yells at it.

The beast stares him down. It's similar to a bear, but modified to be twice as large and much more frightening. Small, curved horns grow out of its head, and there are fangs protruding from its mouth.

The fangs drip, and I realize they're full of poison. Carter steps closer to the beast, trying to ignite its fury. It charges, and I quickly duck back behind the tree, unable to look. I close my eyes, hoping this ends fast.

Carter screams, a sickening, guttural sound that will haunt me forever.

Then everything fades to black.

MY EYES FLUTTER open to the sunlight pouring through the window. I sit up in my bed, alone. I'm a little disappointed that Atlas isn't here.

Then I realize that implies I miss him and shake the thought away.

My phone begins vibrating on my bedside table.

"Hello?"

"Good, you're awake."

Atlas's voice makes me ache, wishing he was here with me. The unearthly sound of Carter's scream is still haunting me.

"Yeah, I just woke up."

"I've been up for a bit. I saw Carter. He's sleeping like the dead now, but he's okay."

I sit up in bed. "He's alive?"

I can almost hear Atlas smiling. "Yeah. He woke up for about ten minutes and demanded answers about what happened. I filled him in, and then he fell back to sleep. He's salty that we followed him, but he'll be fine when he wakes up again. I texted his boss from his phone, telling him he isn't feeling well and needs the day. His boss is pretty chill. Mine, however, is not. So I'm about to head to work."

Luckily, it's my day off, so I don't have worry about those things. "Okay. Thanks for calling me. I'm glad he's okay."

"Me, too. Though I have to admit, I'm disappointed I didn't wake up next to you again."

I'm stunned. Atlas takes my silence as discomfort and says, "You can laugh at me. I know it's foolish."

"No, it's okay." *Tell him I feel the same.* He should know I don't hate him.

"I'd better get to work. I'll see you later."

He hangs up before I can say anything else. My heart aches to see him, especially after the terrifying events we just went through.

Ten minutes later I'm on the road. Five minutes after that, I realize that I have no idea where he works. And didn't he mention having two jobs? Which one would he be at today?

I could drive to his apartment and wait for him to come home, but that could be hours from now. I could ask Carter. I decide that's what I'll do when I get there.

I'm so lost in thought that I don't see the car

speeding through the stop sign on the cross road. There's the sudden jerk of my car flying sideways. Glass shatters, sending glittering shards flying through the air. Tiny pinpricks of cuts burn over my arms and face. My car spins on its side before fully flipping. My heart pounds, and then my head hits the roof. The cracking sound my neck makes is sickening. The pain is so intense, I cry out. Sound seems lost at this moment. My world spins out one last time before I black out.

34

Ophelia

Sixteen Years Old

"WAITING IT OUT isn't going well." I sigh, leaning back against the park bench Milo and I are seated on. There's a bag of kettle corn between us to share. The town's yearly autumn carnival is in full swing, but I don't feel like going through the motions or riding any of the rides.

Milo sips his soda and shrugs. "I never said it would happen fast. I said it would happen eventually."

I groan. "I need to get over him already. There's no use in waiting around for someone who's not here for me. He never texts me anymore, especially not when he's with her. We used to hang out at least a little bit. It's like I'm not even in their friend group now."

Milo glances at me through the curtain of brown hair that's fallen in his eyes. "Sounds like a terrible friend."

I see Moriah and Atlas across the park, in line for the Ferris wheel. His arm is around her, holding her close. She whispers something in his ear. He kisses her.

I look down. Milo sighs, standing up. "Come on."

"Where?"

"I'm done watching you mope over a guy who isn't going to give you the time of day. Yeah, I do think they'll break up. But seriously, he could at least invest a little time in his friendship with you."

Milo reaches for my hand, pulling me from the bench. I look up into his gray eyes. "Where are we going?"

"We're going to enjoy the carnival. It only comes once a year."

I'm not entirely convinced, but Milo is determined. He pays for us to sit at a booth and shoot water guns at targets. Then we move on to a rock-climbing area.

Bit by bit, my thoughts drift away from Atlas and his absence.

Milo pulls me towards the Ferris wheel, and I stop. The line has moved, but Atlas and Moriah are now getting a turn.

"He's over there," I say, jerking my chin to where they're climbing into a car, giggling.

"So what?" Milo smirks. "Your life doesn't have to revolve around him anymore. Let's ride the Ferris wheel and see our beautiful town."

I let Milo lead me to the wheel, his fingers intertwined with mine. I notice he hasn't let go when we reach the boarding area. But I don't say anything. My racing heart forbids me from asking him why.

Because in this moment, it feels good to have someone nearby. Someone whose skin is pressed against mine.

Someone I can feel is real.

We're given a seat, and Milo lets my hand go. Instead, he rests his arm around my shoulders. This gesture isn't new to me—he's done it a few times before—but there's something different about it this time.

Something that leaves butterflies in my stomach.

The wheel begins its spin, slow and steady. I hate heights, but this isn't the worst feeling in the world. Milo pulls me closer and says, "I know you hate being high up, but I think the view is worth it."

I glance at him. The fading sunlight is making him glow golden.

I'm starting to think maybe I've ignored what I could've had by looking at what I thought I wanted.

When the wheel goes down, slow, I reach my hand up to where Milo's is resting on my shoulder and hold onto it. His fingers intertwine with mine as though we've done this a million times before. And when it's time to get off, it feels suddenly cold as we separate and step out onto the platform.

We head off towards the exit, pushing our way through the other passengers, and suddenly he takes my hand again and makes me face him. "Ophelia, there's something I need to tell you."

In his eyes, I see fear. Something that isn't usual for him. I notice his eyes trailing down to my lips, then back to my eyes. I smile softly. "There's something I need to do first," I say.

"What is—" I don't let him finish his sentence

before I kiss him. It's quick, and I'm shaking when I pull away.

His eyes are confused and I'm wondering if I misread the situation, if I'm going to lose the only friend I have left.

But then he grabs me by the waist, one hand holding my chin, and kisses me again, this one full of wanting.

I wrap my arms around his neck, and it feels *right*. When we finally pull away, he smiles. "I was going to say I can't leave here without getting funnel cake... but this was better."

"We can still get funnel cake if you share."

He kisses me again, quickly, and then pulls me towards the food carts. "Let's go."

THE PARK ISN'T particularly busy this time of the morning, despite it being summer. I sit on the bench, watching a couple of joggers pass by.

Atlas walks up, taking a seat next to me.

"We need to talk," he says.

I nod. "I agree."

He's hesitant to speak, but I can tell whatever he wants to say is bothering him. He rubs his hands on his jeans, a sign of nervousness.

"Atlas," I begin. "If you're scared to say it..."

He shakes his head. "I saw you kiss Milo last night at the festival."

That's what this is about? "Okay?"

"His reputation isn't great."

I roll my eyes. "I appreciate your concern, but I can

take care of myself. He's really nice to me. And he's been there for me when you haven't." There. I've said it.

Atlas sighs. "I've messed up. You're my best friend and I've neglected you. And... Moriah told me you used to have a crush on me. You stopped talking to her because I chose her."

The accusations catch me off guard. Not only did Moriah tell him about my feelings—something that wasn't hers to share—but she lied about me. "Atlas... I never stopped talking to either of you. I've tried. But neither of you ever wants to hang out with me anymore. She stopped responding to my texts altogether. And you cancel plans anytime you actually make any with me. I never cut either of you off."

"I know I've canceled plans a lot lately. I feel terrible about that. But Moriah said—"

"Moriah says a lot of things that aren't true," I snap. "She's not honest and she isn't kind. At least not to me. I never stopped talking to her. She stopped talking to me first. I've sent so many unanswered texts. I stopped when I realized she was done trying to talk to me."

Atlas looks hesitant to believe me. I get up from the bench, looking at him. "And yes, Atlas. I did have a crush on you. Moriah knew that *before* she ever dated you. She chose to cross that line, and I still chose to be friends with both of you. I don't care about that now because I'm happy with Milo. But that's the kind of person Moriah is. Whether you want to believe me or not is up to you."

I don't stay long enough to find out if he does. I turn and leave, walking away from Atlas.

Leaving a piece of my heart cracked and broken.

I shake my head as hot tears burn my eyes. I have Milo. He came into my life with perfect timing.

Maybe he's all I need for now.

I expect Atlas to follow behind me. To stop me from walking away.

A part of me hopes he'll be behind me when I turn and look. But he's gone from the bench and I see him walking towards the parking lot, to his old truck.

This isn't over. I know it isn't over.

35

Atlas

MOST DAYS, I hate my jobs. But today, my yard work job provides a welcome distraction. Here, I can think about anything else besides what happened last night. My boss, Ricky, is normally super thorough, but today he seems oddly relaxed. He sits on the tailgate of his truck, eating a sandwich while I lean against the rake, sipping some water.

My phone rings and I pull it out of my pocket. The number is unfamiliar, but I answer anyway.

"Hello?"

"Is this Atlas Jameson?"

"Yes. May I ask whom I'm speaking to?"

The man clears his throat. "This is Officer Parks with the Ellis County Police Department. I'm calling to inform you that Ophelia Maddox has been in an accident."

My heart goes cold. I can't lose her, too.

"I'm sorry, what?"

"Ophelia has no emergency contacts listed, and you were the last person she had an incoming call from. We've tried to contact her father, but he isn't answering."

"He's at work and can't have his phone on his person. What hospital is she at?"

Ricky glances over at me curiously. Officer Parks says, "North Baptist. I am unaware of her condition. The other person involved walked away from the scene unharmed, but they've been taken into custody for questioning as it appears they may have been under the influence of something."

"Thank you, Officer. I will go see her as soon as I can get away. I appreciate the call."

"Yes, sir. I do hope your friend recovers. Stay safe out there."

Ice courses through my veins at the thought that Ophelia isn't okay. I'm frozen in place, unsure of what to do. Unsure if Ricky will be okay with me leaving before my shift is over.

Ricky has approached now. "Go on. I can finish here. I overheard enough to know it's important."

"Are you sure?"

"Yeah, I'm sure. Who is it?"

"My friend I've just recently reconnected with. We were best friends as kids. She's been in an accident."

He takes the rake from my hand. "Go see her. She needs you."

I don't let him tell me again. I thank him and run to my truck. I put the address of the hospital into my phone, send a quick text to Carter, and start driving.

Time suddenly seems to be moving achingly slowly. I need to know she's okay.

I can't lose her now.

If the dream had let us wake up together... would this have happened? I shake my head. I can't think like that. I don't know why we didn't all wake up in the same room, though, since we were all in the same dream.

Forty-five minutes later, I arrive at the hospital. It's busy, the parking lot nearly full. I park and rush inside to the front desk. The receptionist looks calm, despite the air of urgency all around her.

"I'm here to see a patient who was just admitted."

"Your name?"

"Atlas Jameson."

The receptionist types something on the computer. "Name of the patient?"

"Ophelia Maddox."

"How are you related?"

"I'm a friend."

The receptionist frowns. "Sorry, but only next of kin can go see any patient immediately."

"The police called me. They couldn't get ahold of her dad, and it's not likely they will within the next twelve hours. I'm who they called, and if you don't believe me, I can show you the call log on my phone."

The receptionist looks uncertain, but she types some more things into the computer. I hold my phone out to her, hoping they will know that this number belongs to an officer. The receptionist types some more, and the seconds stretch on agonizingly.

Every moment I waste here at the front desk is a moment Ophelia is alone.

The receptionist glances around, then back at me. "Room 220B. She's listed as unconscious, in critical condition. I didn't let you get by if you're asked."

"Thank you," I say.

Critical condition.

I rush towards the elevators, reading signs to guide me to the right place. I find the room after some wrong turns, and find I'm not the only one waiting outside.

There's a girl with pink hair sitting in a chair outside the room. The girl from the café. She must be friends with Ophelia. She looks up, seeming unsurprised to see me standing there. Her bright blue eyes are rimmed with tears.

"How is she?" I ask.

The girl shakes her head. "The doctors won't let me in. They said I'm not an emergency contact or relative."

"An officer called me."

A nurse exits the door and looks right at me. She frowns. "You said an officer called you? Atlas Jameson?"

"Yes, ma'am."

Pink Hair looks at me. "She'll be happy to know you're here. But why didn't they contact her dad?"

"I was the last person she spoke to on the phone, about twenty minutes before the accident. Her dad hasn't answered any of the calls yet."

Pink Hair pushes up from the chair. "Please take care of her."

"Of course."

"I'm Reya, Ophelia's best friend. I've heard all about you, Atlas Jameson. Ophelia has told me everything."

Everything? I can't tell if that means she knows about the dreams, or that she knows Ophelia and I have been talking again after all these years.

I glance at the nurse, who is waiting for me by the door. "When you're ready, Mr. Jameson, you can enter the room."

I nod once, then trail my eyes back to Reya. "I don't know what Ophelia has told you. But she means the world to me. And I'm grateful she's let me back in her life. I promise you; I will take care of her. I can't... I can't lose her again."

The words slice my heart. Waking up next to her, saving her from drowning, seeing her in the forest with the black butterflies... It meant everything to me. But now, she lies here in this hospital fighting for her life. And the idea that I could lose her for good, just when we've started to be friends again is tearing me up inside.

Reya still seems hesitant. I can't blame her for not trusting me. But she waves me off. "Go see her. Then you can tell me what's going on."

I don't wait for her to change her mind. I enter the room. The only sound accompanying my steps is the beeping of monitors.

Ophelia looks barely alive. Her skin is ashen. A purple bruise mars her jaw. There are IVs and tubes attached to her arms. One is attached to her left pointer finger. A mask is over her nose and mouth, helping her breathe.

Despite all of this, the sound of the machines beeping tells me she's alive.

The nurse returns. "We still cannot get ahold of her father. She's in a coma. And we're not sure she'll come out of it. There doesn't appear to be head trauma, but her heart is weak."

My breath hitches in my throat. "I'll see if I can get ahold of her dad. Until he's aware, I would like to stay here."

The nurse nods. "Visiting hours end at 9 p.m., but you can stay past that, as her emergency contact."

I don't say I wasn't an emergency contact. I was just a chance call the officer hoped would bring answers.

I take a seat next to the bed, scooting the chair closer. I take Ophelia's hand, the one that's untouched by cords and wires. "I know you're probably scared," I say softly. "But please fight. I can't..." I exhale, feeling my resolve slowly wane. "I can't lose you, Ophelia."

I close my eyes, resting my head on the bed next to her hand. "Don't leave me."

After some time, I try to call her dad. But there's no response. Needing to stretch my legs and get some air, I wander back out into the hall. Reya looks up, her eyes full of questions, so I fill her in on what's going on. She doesn't seem thrilled when I go back into the room.

I text Carter more information, as well as the location of the hospital.

As day shifts into night, I take a seat on the chair again, resting my eyes. The nurses have come in many times, checking Ophelia's vitals. Checking for any sign of life.

When the visiting hours end, I don't leave. I can't leave her like this.

To my own detriment, I fall asleep on the chair.

36

Atlas

Seventeen Years Old

THE BEACH HOUSE isn't at all what I expected it to be. Moriah and her family enjoy going on boats and jet skis. But the water is murky and cold. I enjoy sitting on the dock, listening to the water move in the stillness.

Moriah takes a seat next to me. "I know you're upset about Ophelia, but I'm sure she'll come around."

"Moriah... have you been ignoring Ophelia's texts?"

Moriah is silent beside me for a long time. I almost think she's not going to answer, when she finally sighs. "Sometimes I was busy. So I did forget some texts. Why?"

"Ophelia feels like we didn't put any effort into including her. That's why she pulled away. And she's right. I would cancel on her constantly if you wanted something from me. I never made time for her."

Moriah shifts away from me. "Okay, well, when

you have a girlfriend, you can't always give your girl best friend all the time she wants."

"She was my best friend before we dated. And before I ever met you. I can at least give her a little time. We could've all gone to do things together. But we didn't even try."

Moriah stands up. "I don't understand why you're so hung up on this—unless you have feelings for her, too."

"What?"

"Do you have, or have you ever had feelings for Ophelia?"

I shake my head. "I don't think so. I don't have feelings for her right now. I'm with you. I don't know about before. I never really thought about it. But I know I feel bad that I never made her a priority."

The skies begin to darken behind Moriah. A storm must be coming.

I rise to my feet. "When we get back home, we have to give her time."

"I don't want to, okay?"

"Why not?"

"Because she has feelings for you. I don't buy that she's over you and with Milo now. Maybe he's a distraction, but they're not compatible. I'm not comfortable hanging around her when I know how she feels."

I cross my arms. "You apparently knew how she felt before we started dating and that didn't stop you from dating me."

Moriah huffs. "You're blaming me?"

"No, I'm saying that you knew this would happen."

Suddenly everything feels very still inside me. "Honestly, I think we need to take a break. I'll call my mom to come pick me up. You finish out the vacation with your family."

Moriah shakes her head incredulously. "You're leaving me?"

"I don't think we should see each other right now. We need to take a break."

"So that's it? Just because some old crush Ophelia had on you comes to light, you want to end everything we've had for two years?"

I shake my head, but the anger inside of me is rising, threatening to break to the surface. "I'm not trying to end everything. I'm saying that I've ignored my best friend for two years to be with you. And I'm realizing I should've done more to be there for her."

Moriah crosses her arms, standing in the way of me making it back to the house. "I am your girlfriend. I'm not comfortable with you having a girl best friend. Does that mean nothing to you?"

All my pent-up anger bursts out now before I can stop it. "You knew she was my best friend before we started dating." My voice is louder than I intend it to be, but I can't stop now. "Ophelia and I both trusted you. You broke her heart and, in the process, you made me break hers, too."

"If you have a crush on her, just come out and say it already. You obviously want her more than me."

"At the moment, I wish I'd known she had feelings for me because then maybe I wouldn't be stuck here dealing with yet another mess you've created."

The words are out before I can stop them. Moriah's

eyes widen, as if she's been slapped in the face.

She storms off without another word. I lean against the post on the dock. I stay rooted to this spot for what feels like forever. I'm scared to face what awaits me in the house. Eventually, though, I have to get home, meaning I have to face them all. I turn away from the ocean, glancing up at the clouds forming in the sky.

When I get back to the house, Moriah's mom is there. "Honey, you don't have to leave. Sometimes arguments happen."

I force a smile. "Thank you, but I think it would be best if Moriah and I had some space. I want her to enjoy her vacation."

A loud clap of thunder shakes the house, startling all of us. Moriah's mom pales. "Oh no. I need to stop Moriah from going out on the water."

"What?"

"She said she was going to go jet skiing to cool off. I know that thunder won't deter her from going."

I follow Mrs. Reyes and we run towards the dock. Moriah is already out on the water as rain begins to fall.

"MORIAH!" Mrs. Reyes calls out.

But she's too far. And suddenly it's raining, hard. We start waving like crazy, shouting her name. Rain is soaking through our clothes now. The wind has come up, and the surface of the ocean turns choppy.

Everything that happens next is a blur. The jet ski toppling over. Moriah trying to swim back, her head bobbing frantically above the waves. The water churning around her, taking her under.

Mrs. Reyes screams. I run to get Mr. Reyes, who's still in the house. Mrs. Reyes pulls out her phone and calls the police. I rush back down to the dock, with Mr. Reyes right behind me. Moriah has yet to surface.

The first responders arrive quickly in their vehicles, and a harbor patrol boat appears shortly afterward. There's a lot of commotion and activity, both on shore and out on the water. I wait on the shoreline with Moriah's parents; the rain is still pouring down with no remorse. When they pull Moriah from the ocean, she's not breathing. The paramedics rush her to the ambulance, her mother and father rushing with her. I wait on the porch of the house, pacing.

But I already know she's gone when Mrs. Reyes wails, crumpling to the ground, calling out for Moriah. She begins sobbing uncontrollably.

I know she's gone when Mr. Reyes, through his own tears, comes over to the porch and assures me that none of this is my fault.

I know she's gone when the ambulance takes her away, its lights no longer flashing, the sirens silent. Mr. Reyes helps his wife into the car before they follow the ambulance, away from the beach house.

Away from me.

I call my mom to come get me, though I'm barely aware of what I'm doing. My body is numb; my mind is beyond rational thought. I'm too shocked to speak at first when my mom asks me what's wrong.

And then I'm sobbing, trying to explain everything that's happened. She's calm, but I can hear the emotion in her voice when she tells my dad he needs to come get me. She keeps me on the phone, but I don't speak.

I'm crying, then I'm not. I've cried all I can. I look

out to the ocean, watching as the rain finally slows down to a stop. Watching as the weather no longer looks dangerous or threatening.

But it doesn't matter if the storm's stopped now because Moriah is gone.

37

Ophelia

IT'S DARK WHEN I first wake up. Then I realize I'm not awake in reality. Lanterns glow around me. I sit up, though I find it's achingly hard to do in this ball gown I'm in.

I rub at my eyes, then pull my hands away, puzzled. They're coated in a layer of glitter. I rise to my feet after some struggle. I walk around this strange place, though there's not much to walk around in. It's a dome of sorts. As I go closer to the walls, I realize they're tree branches, overlapping one another.

"Ophelia."

The whispers sound near me, yet echo in this dome-like structure. I freeze where I stand, waiting to find what spoke my name.

Or waiting for it to find me.

There's a slight breeze that blows my hair, chilling me.

I'm startled when I turn, finding Rook sitting on a ledge about ten feet off the ground.

I don't acknowledge him, not wanting to give him the satisfaction of my fear.

I begin walking along the walls, feeling my way around the tangle of branches. Everything is sealed shut.

In the center of the dome is a floating object made of flowers and branches, shaped like an anatomical heart.

"It's beautiful, isn't it?"

I'm startled by the sound of Rook's voice. He's hovering behind me now, cloaked in shadows, as he always is. His pale orbs for eyes seem dimmer than usual.

This close, he almost seems more human than shadow.

"What do you want?" I demand.

"Ah, you ask the wrong question," he says. "You already know what I want. You should be asking why I saved your nightmare for last."

"This can't be my nightmare. I'm in a dome made of trees, covered in glitter and wearing a ball gown."

"You have a very poetic soul, my sweet Ophelia. I took a little creative freedom with designing this. That heart is yours. Locked away in this place to keep it safe, just as you always do. You don't like to let people close to you. You don't want them seeing the contents of your heart. I admire and applaud that."

Where's Atlas?"

The sudden absence of Atlas has my heart, the one in my chest, beating rapidly. Every time we were cast into a dream, we were together.

The lack of him here is frightening.

Rook chuckles. "Oh, he'll get to this place eventually, but there will be many challenges he has to face, as this is not only your nightmare. I don't know what sort of bond you two have, but his newest fears are entangled with yours. It will be a challenge to escape this one, I can assure you of that."

"Why are you doing this?"

"I already told you why I'm doing this."

I shake my head, taking a step closer to him. "I mean, why are you putting me in a safe situation? You've basically put me in a gilded cage. The only way out is if Atlas saves me. Why am I not fighting for my own soul?"

Rook laughs again, as though this is something humorous and not serious. "My sweet Ophelia, you *are* fighting for your own soul. But if I'm honest..." He lowers himself to the ground, the shadows all around him dissipating. His face is covered by a mask, only his glowing eyes visible. The rest of him is more human than he's appeared in the time we've been dealing with him. His skin is still dark from the shadows, but now, I am less afraid. "I don't want to hurt you. You're special. This was my loophole, my way of not bringing harm upon you."

I'm about to ask more questions, but he's gone. I look around this cage I'm stuck in, stare at the centerpiece that represents my heart.

I rush to the walls, feeling for any sort of opening. Any weak point that I can break away. Then I can escape and find Atlas.

I'm no damsel in distress, waiting for my prince.

Each branch is tightly woven, making the walls impenetrable. I collapse to the ground, my ball gown pooling out from under me. The hope that there might be a crack in the wall was all I had.

It never can be that simple.

Without Atlas here, I don't know how I'll escape. And if our fears are intertwining, I don't know what that means for either of us.

The only way Atlas will enter this place is if he goes to sleep.

I don't remember falling asleep. I don't remember much before entering this dream. Was it night? Did I fall ill and take a nap?

I pace around the heart Rook claims is mine. It beats, though not fast or strong. It's almost like it's fighting just to keep beating. As though there's something weakening it. Maybe there's a time limit.

There's an ache in my own chest, but I ignore it for now. Whatever awaits Atlas, I can only hope he'll be able to fight it to find me.

38

Ophelia

Sixteen Years Old

WAKING UP THIS morning was normal. But then I started getting frantic texts from Atlas's and my mutual acquaintances, asking me if I'd heard the news. The hair stood up on the back of my neck. *What news?* More texts come in from classmates, asking me if I was doing okay.

And then Atlas's voicemail.

He's choking on sobs, something I've never heard.

"Ophelia... I'm sorry. Moriah's gone. She's gone. Please call me back. I need you."

I called ten times.

All calls went to voicemail, as if his phone wasn't even on.

My father was home, a rarity, when I went downstairs. He held me when I cried. Comforted me until it was time for him to go to work. He offered to use one of his days off. But I knew how hard it was for him to bring himself to do those things. Drowning in his work was the only way he coped with life. And I didn't want to burden him more by keeping him home.

I would rather sit alone, anyway.

I waited for Atlas to call me back. I texted him many times, hoping for something.

But a response never came.

A couple of days, then a week.

Then it's the funeral. I find Atlas in the pews, sitting alone near the back. I sit next to him, but he doesn't acknowledge me.

"I tried to call you. I've texted you a thousand times. I don't know if you're mad that I missed your call when I was asleep, or if you're grieving so hard that it hurts. But I'm here for you."

"It's my fault," he murmurs. "We were arguing."

"You and Moriah?"

He nods slowly, almost uncertainly. "We argued. I asked for a break and I was going to call my mom to get me. I didn't want to stay. There was some thunder, but she went out on the water anyway. She wanted to scare me or maybe get away from me. It's my fault."

I shake my head, taking his hand. "It's not your fault. We both know how impulsive Moriah is—was."

I cringe. This comforting talk is already off to a terrible start. Still, I continue. "She was stubborn as hell. You loved her for that. She probably wanted to cool off. She wouldn't have done that to cause you any fear, and she probably didn't think she'd get hurt."

Atlas shivers, despite the church being quite warm. "I don't know. I don't know anything. I failed her. It's my fault."

My heart feels like it's breaking. I had hoped to fix things with Moriah. I wanted to be friends. I didn't know why she stopped talking to me, but I wanted to fix everything between the three of us and go back to being the way we were. Maybe even bring Milo along sometimes.

But the pain of everything swells inside me now, burying a seed of misery deep in my chest. I begin to sob. Atlas doesn't move to comfort me. He doesn't hold me close, or even hold my hand, like I did for him moments before. He rises from the pew and leaves me be.

I realize then that we're broken beyond repair. Neither of them valued me as a friend.

Milo finds me moments later and does what I had wanted Atlas to do. He holds me, whispers comforting words in my ear. He kisses my cheek, my head, my hands. We stay in the back during the funeral. He holds my hand while he drives us to the burial site.

I stay back when everyone drops a flower onto Moriah's casket. She wouldn't want me here. I realize that now.

"Milo," I whisper. "Take me home."

He doesn't hesitate. He guides me to his car and takes off out of the parking lot. He doesn't expect me to say anything or fill the silence.

"Atlas was a real asshole to you," he says. "I saw you sitting with him. And the moment you needed comfort, he ran off."

I lean my head against the window. "He's hurting. He blames himself. I don't want to talk about it, though."

Milo doesn't push to talk about anything concerning the funeral. When we pull up to my house, he sees that the lights are off and the driveway is empty, and he sighs. "Your dad isn't home?"

"When is he ever?"

"I don't like leaving you alone."

I shrug. "I've gotten used to being alone. You know that much."

He leans over, tucking stray strands of my hair behind my ear. "As long as I'm around, you're not going to be alone. I know your dad won't like it, but I'd like to come inside. You can shower and take a nap. I'll stay on the couch and watch TV. Just until he comes home. Then I'll leave."

I want to tell him no, to make him go home and not worry about me. But we're too far beyond that point already. I nod, unable to say anything.

He gets out of his car and comes around, helping me out and guiding me to the door. I pull my keys from my purse and let us inside.

"I will sit here on the couch," he says, looking toward the living room. "You shower and take a nap. It will help."

I brush past him and go upstairs, doing what he says. I start the water for the shower and peel off my clothes.

When the hot water hits my skin, it's like magic. I scrub myself clean, washing off the taint of the funeral, soothing the wounds to my heart and my soul, imagining the hurt and the pain washing down the drain. I let the water wash over me, soothe me, renew me.

I don't know how long I'm in the shower, but when I finally get out, my skin is red from the hot water. I don't care. I wrap my wet hair in a towel and pull on my pajamas.

It's almost therapeutic, sitting on my bed, combing my hair. I count the times the comb passes through my long waves, but I eventually lose count. Still, I comb until there's no knots or tangles from the wind outside at the gravesite.

After all of that, I braid my hair slowly, then climb underneath the blankets on my bed. I hate that Milo is right, but I needed this time to process and exist in my room alone.

I try to sleep, but every time I close my eyes, there are flashbacks of good memories with Moriah, as well as the bad. I sit up, sobbing into my hands.

"Hey, shh. It's okay."

Milo sits next to me; he probably rushed up here when he heard me crying. His arms wrap around me, pulling me into his chest.

I don't say anything to him. I can't say a word between all the sobbing.

When I've finally shed every last tear I have left, I'm beyond exhausted.

"Moriah did a lot of things wrong to you, but that doesn't mean she wasn't someone who meant something to you. It doesn't mean you can't grieve the loss of who she used to be. At one time, she was your closest friend. No matter where you stood recently, she still meant something." Milo finishes his speech by kissing my forehead.

I nod slowly. "I never would've wanted this to happen. She didn't deserve this. But what's worse is I'm so numb about her death. These tears are for Atlas. I guess I just thought he would need me again. That he would want me to comfort him. That he'd want to comfort me. We both lost someone who meant a lot to us."

Hot tears prick behind my eyes, threatening to break free yet again. I blink, hoping to chase them away.

Milo frowns in the way he always does when it comes to Atlas. I know there's a part of him that worries that my heart will never fully belong here, with him. That it will always belong to Atlas.

I lean up and kiss Milo softly, a reassurance.

"He doesn't deserve your tears," he murmurs when I pull away.

"Maybe not. But that doesn't mean I don't have tears to cry."

"I should let you sleep."

I sigh. The silence of the house is getting louder, pressing in around me. "You could stay with me."

"I don't feel like being murdered by your dad when he does eventually make it home tonight. But I'm a phone call away. I'll have my phone by my bed, ready to come here whenever you need."

He kisses me again before standing, tucking me into the bed. He closes the door behind him as he leaves the room. I hear him shut the front door, then the sound of his car pulling away.

My body is exhausted; my eyes finally fall shut. Maybe I can sleep away the grief and the heartache.

Maybe I'll wake up and it will all be a nightmare. Atlas and I won't be fighting and Moriah will still be alive.

But life doesn't work like that.

Slowly, I drift away into a nightmare-filled sleep.

39

Atlas

THE SOUND OF wolves howling nearby wakes me up. The night sky above is suspended in an eventide phase—somewhat dark, somewhat light. Stars twinkle, and the moon is a waxing crescent.

"Where the hell are we?"

Carter's voice startles me. He's already on his feet. I sit up. "Another dream world."

He groans. "I faced my fear. Why do I have to come back? I literally died. I'm exhausted."

I look around. The wolves are still howling in the distance.

We're in a clearing. The woods ahead of us are thick, with vines and ivy growing on the trees. It's growing chilly as the darker parts of the sky bleed into the lighter ones.

"It's Ophelia's dream," I breathe, my words forming wisps in the air.

Carter straightens up. "We have to find her. This may be the key to pulling her out of her coma."

"Not only that, but it won't look good if the nurses come into the room and can't wake me up, either."

Carter marches towards the woods. "She's obviously going to be somewhere in there. Let's go."

The wolves' howling grows more powerful the moment our feet enter the dark forest. The air is colder here, and any light left in the sky is snuffed out.

We keep walking, despite this. I have to find Ophelia. There's no light, nothing to guide us. Only the sounds of our feet crunching leaves on the path and wolves howling every so often.

Finally, Carter says, "This is getting darker and darker. I think we should stick close together."

"What, you want to hold hands?"

"No, dumbass. Hold onto my shoulder or something."

I reach out, and my hand collides with Carter, but not his shoulder. I smack his face, and he grunts. His hand grabs my wrist and guides my hand to his shoulder. "It's not rocket science."

"It is when I can't see anything."

We continue walking through the darkness, until it slowly becomes less dark. It's not light by any means, but now I can see the outline of Carter and not have to hold his shoulder.

We stop for a breather, backs to a tree in case a wolf decides to pop out of the bushes looking for a snack.

I finally say the words on my mind. "Why would she be this deep in the woods?"

"I'm not sure. But I think we need to get inside her

head. What are her fears? How does this resemble something inside her?"

Of all the years I've known Ophelia, the one thing I know for certain is how hard it is to get her out of her shell. The woods must be her outer shell. The deeper into the trees we go, the closer we get to her.

40

Rook

I TOLD HER I want her safe, and that is true. But what I didn't say—couldn't say—is that I want to punish Atlas more than anything. And I have to maintain appearances to the Shadow Council, which is why I targeted his ridiculous roommate, too.

I also discovered that Ophelia's best friend, Reya, has a protection over her mind. It's the reason I've yet to break through and manipulate her nightmares. Something about the challenge intrigues me. I don't plan to give on her yet. But the more fruitful path has been the other three.

Reya's mind games will have to wait.

In haunting them, I've learned a lot.

I've learned bringing Ophelia and Atlas together again was not the painful experience I expected it to be for them.

And that Carter is Moriah's cousin. That was never something I was aware of.

And I've learned Reya's dreams have the best essence, the strongest aura. I've yet to be able to unlock them, though. I've tried to make my way through her mind, finding her fears and manipulating them. But nothing works. She's locked tighter than the cage Ophelia is in right now.

I will have to try harder, but for now my focus is on the three I've been able to manipulate.

Now, as I search for Atlas in the woods, I can't help but wonder how his newest fears are entangled with Ophelia's.

Ophelia is scared to let people into her heart, to give them a chance to break it. But there's also another, fainter fear buried in the depths of her mind that I can't fully reach. I've never been unable to read someone's mind.

Atlas's newest fear is no surprise, I must admit. He's no longer scared of drowning. He's scared to lose Ophelia.

I soar above the trees in shadow form, weaving up and down, in and out, trying to find my mark.

Atlas and Carter are resting, backs against a tree. Smart, considering there are other things lurking in these woods. I sense the pack of white wolves tucked further away, not minding that two human snacks are within reach, sitting ducks.

I can't interfere now, not that I would. I can only observe what I have set in motion. I did speak to Ophelia, though, even though it's against the rules. But screw rules and regulations. She needed to know I will never harm her.

The guilt about her falling off the boat in Atlas's

dream eats at me. *He* was supposed to fall off. He was supposed to either sink or swim. I didn't care much about what happened to him.

But Ophelia fell, and he dove in after her. I let him live because he saved her. But I will no longer be merciful to him: this is my chance to finally end him.

The roommate is collateral damage, though I'll spare him if he makes it to the end of this nightmare. He deserves something; it's not his fault he got dragged into this.

I don't stay observing them too long. The game is already afoot. I take off back to the shelter, back to Ophelia.

I will protect her there, though from afar. I will not interfere again, for the consequences from the Council will be harsh. They've already ruined my life, turning me into this monster. I don't need to see what else they have in store for me if I fall out of line again.

I land on a ledge in the dome, watching as Ophelia walks around its perimeter, pressing her fingers against the walls, feeling for a way out. She doesn't know that the walls will come down if she lets them. She doesn't know that the people she wants inside can enter.

The poetry of this place is as simple as discovering oneself. It's simply complex, I suppose you could say. I settle on the ledge, wishing that I could reveal all the secrets to Ophelia.

Wishing that there was a universe in which she would open her eyes and see me.

But only my true love can free me from the Curse of Shadows. And only that love will be able to see me for who I am.

Or who I was.

I don't know if speaking in past tense is more painful than using the present tense. Past and present no longer have any meaning for me. Everything blurs together and time no longer exists in these nightmares.

So, for now, I rest. I wait for Atlas and his roommate to arrive.

I wait to see what will transpire.

41

Ophelia

MY HANDS RUN across the rough bark of the branches that make my shelter. I never get a splinter, though the wood is rough enough to give me one.

I close my eyes, trying to breathe. Center myself.

"I know you're watching me," I say out loud. "I know you feel protective of me. But I don't understand why."

I can sense Rook all around me, yet I don't see him. Not yet. But he's there. And there's something familiar in the way he's treating me. "We have a connection. You've been able to invade my mind. It shouldn't be a one-way street."

His voice is soft in my head, almost nonexistent.

"Oh, really?"

Yes.

No other information is offered. I didn't really expect it to be. I turn, trying to determine where he's hiding. Then I spot a ledge higher up in the dome, where the shadows seem restless.

"You don't have to hide from me. Maybe if we could talk like normal people—"

His shadowy form lands six feet away, facing of me. "What about me makes you think I'm a normal person?"

His words are bitter, almost regretful.

"Maybe you weren't always like this," I say. "Maybe there was more to you before."

He doesn't respond. I bite my lip, forcing my eyes to focus where his should be. All that exists is shadow. No eyes, nose, or lips where they should be. No expression.

Only hidden features in the dark void.

"Why do you need to cause this pain? There has to be more than just... nightmares and souls for you."

He laughs bitterly as I take a step closer to where he stands. "You assume that everything is black and white."

I don't step any closer, but I do begin to walk back and forth in front of him, pacing as I think out loud. "Maybe it isn't black and white, but I don't think this is all there is. There's a motive behind all of this."

"You ascribe too much humanity to a shadow creature like me."

I stop pacing and face him again. "You sound human. You look mostly human. There has to be a human heart beating inside your chest."

"Ah, my sweet Ophelia, you always want to find the humanity in something. But I'm afraid you give me too much credit. I will admit, at one point I was a human. I did have a human heart beating in my chest. And I loved someone. But then I lost her. I lost her because of my own stubbornness. But that was my past, and this is my present and future."

"If you were human... how are you now this shadow creature?"

"The Shadow Council found me. And they showed me what I was capable of after being doubted my entire life. Limitless power and endless possibilities. I couldn't resist."

"No."

He tilts his head. I imagine if he had features on his face, an eyebrow would be raised.

"No?"

I cross my arms. "I don't believe you. I don't believe you enjoy inflicting pain on people. Why else would you have put me here to protect me? Why else would you prevent me from fighting my fears?"

He appears closer now. I didn't notice him stepping towards me. Maybe he didn't. "I am protecting you, but you will still have to face your fear. There are limits to what my powers can do. I still have to follow the rules of the Shadow Council. But there are reasons I want to protect you. Reasons I will not tell the likes of you."

I stare hard at him, at his shadowy face, puzzled by his uncaring attitude. Deep down there is more. I know there is. The longer I stare, the more things grow clearer. I focus.

I refuse to believe he wants to be this way. Something about him feels... familiar.

And then things grow even clearer.

For a moment, there's something taking shape in the shadows. Something changing on the outside of his skin. The dark wisps are lightening, transforming.

Maybe even breaking apart.

He looks down at his arms, at his legs. "What are you doing to me?"

"I'm choosing to see a human, not a soulless void of shadows who claims he wants to hunt down humans and consume their souls. Because I know there's more to it than all of this."

"Wait." He backs up, but it's already too late. Something about him is shifting, changing.

The shadows are breaking.

Eyes become clear.

Gray as an unforgiving thunderstorm.

The shadows fall away, and in their place is someone I never thought I would see again.

Someone whose heart I broke in high school.

"Milo?"

42

Ophelia

Seventeen Years Old

I GLANCE AROUND the café, waiting anxiously for Milo. He said he had some news. I sip slowly on the latte I ordered while I wait.

When Milo does finally arrive, he goes to order coffee, then turns and finds me sitting in the back booth, our usual spot.

"Thanks for coming," he says.

"Why wouldn't I?"

His eyes shift slightly as he pauses, considering his words. Finally, he takes my hands in his. "My family is moving. Before school starts. I'm going to do senior year at a new school. Unfortunately, it's in an entirely different state."

The words are like arrows to the chest. I lean back, my hands slipping from his. "What do you mean you're moving?"

"I'm sorry. I didn't know until a few days ago. The day of the funeral. But I couldn't ruin your evening more than it already was with that news. And then I chickened out the other few times I had chances."

"The night you promised to be there for me no matter what, you already knew this was temporary?"

He looks down, his face contorted with guilt. "I did. But I'm telling you now because we only have a couple of weeks left together."

"It sucks. But we can make this work."

Tears burn behind my eyes, but I am determined not to let them fall. I keep my emotions hidden now, behind the walls I've built. I *do* think we can make it work. It would take a lot of effort, but I'm willing to put that into us.

Milo leans back in the booth. "I don't want to put you through a long-distance relationship, either. My older sister had a long-distance relationship and it was horrible. Her boyfriend ended up cheating on her."

Another knife to the heart. "Do you not trust me?"

"I trust you fully. The problem isn't trust. It's the pain of being so far apart. There would be no end in sight because I can't guarantee I could move back any more than you could guarantee you'd move to see me."

Everything hurts. My heart, as it breaks apart. My eyes, as they burn with the hot tears I refuse to cry. My ribs, holding my heart together despite the cracks that mar it.

"I'm not willing to stay together for a few weeks just to break up later," I tell him. "If you don't want to do long distance, I can respect that. But I'm not going to pretend everything is okay for two weeks and then let you go."

"But—"

I hold my hand up. "I'm respecting your decisions, Milo. I appreciate the love you have shown me and I appreciate how you've held me together when I've wanted to break. But I can't stay in this when I know it's going to lead to a dead end."

Milo sighs. "We could have the best two weeks of our lives, though. Today doesn't have to be the end of everything."

"Yes, it does. Do you understand how selfish this is of you?"

Milo's eyes widen. "Selfish? You're saying I'm selfish?"

"You gave me hope that there could be someone else to hold my heart. You came into my life when everything around me was falling apart. You have held me together for a couple of months and I appreciate that. But now you want me to pretend for a few more weeks that things will always be this way."

"I'm selfish? For keeping your heart safe while you love someone else from a distance?"

I shake my head. So this is what it's like to really lose everything. "My heart was yours the moment I promised it to you, Milo."

"I'm sorry," he says. I can tell he means it. But it's too late to fix this.

"Me too."

I rise from the booth, leaving my latte and my heart behind. I keep the sobs buried in my chest as I walk home. When I pass people I know, I plaster a fake smile on my face, never showing how I'm really feeling.

Part of me hoped Milo would follow me. But I knew in my heart he wouldn't. He wouldn't chase me down and try to make everything right again. I was on my own this time.

I didn't let the tears fall when I turned down my street and saw my dad's car in the driveway, a very rare occurrence for this time of day.

I didn't cry when I went inside and my dad greeted me with a smile and a hug. I did hold on tighter for a moment, but not long enough for him to question anything.

I didn't cry while we ate dinner together; I kept it together so that we could have a conversation.

I didn't cry while I hugged my dad goodbye before his night shift, waving from the doorway as he pulled out of the driveway.

Only when I'm safe in my room, alone in the house, do I let the tears fall.

43

Atlas

CARTER IS BELTING showtunes at the top of his lungs. And I'm about to murder him.

"What if all that racket makes it impossible to find her?"

Carter pauses for a moment, glaring at me. "You know I hate the dark, especially when it's quiet. I need to fill the space with something."

"You couldn't possibly have any better music in your mental playlist?"

"Better? What do you mean? The musicals I follow are iconic."

I'm about to argue when I notice that there is a faint light ahead. It's almost imperceptible, but it exists.

"Carter, look!"

He looks ahead, and I know he sees it, too. We run towards it. It grows brighter as we get closer, until we're finally in a clearing.

But the clearing is not empty.

There's a large dome reaching for the heavens, made of branches and vines, tightly woven together and definitely impenetrable.

"She has to be in there," I say.

Carter moves closer to the dome and begins to investigate, running his hand along the walls.

"They're rough, but there are no spaces or cracks between them. Nothing big enough to pry open and fight through."

"Ophelia!" I yell, hoping she might hear me from inside.

But it's no use. She can't hear me.

"Ophelia is busy," a deep voice says. I turn, looking for Rook.

But he's nowhere in sight.

"Show yourself."

"I'm afraid I can't do that. You see, your darling Ophelia figured out my identity. And that means my shadows will no longer cloak me. I don't need you two learning who I am before you're supposed to."

Carter and I share a look. Carter clears his throat. "Well, mysterious voice, can you give us a hint as to how we can get inside?"

"Unfortunately, you can't fight to get inside. There's really nothing you can do at this point. It is up to Ophelia to decide whether you will be allowed to enter or not."

"How am I supposed to save her if she can't hear me?"

Rook laughs, a mirthless sound that echoes around the clearing. "I wouldn't assume she can't hear you. Maybe you aren't trying hard enough to hear her call to *you*. You were never one to pay her enough attention, now, were you, Atlas? You see, I'm safely inside the dome with her, and you hear me just fine. Try harder."

I'm confused by what he's getting at, but I turn to Carter, hoping he'll know what's going on. But he shrugs. "Whatever your history is, that's between you and her. Maybe you have sins to atone for."

"You already know the story."

Rook gives a deep, echoing sigh. "This is getting quite tiresome. I am bored of you two. I am going back to talk to sweet Ophelia now. I'm sure you'll find a way in. Hopefully it's before the doctors come back to her hospital room and are unable to wake Atlas."

I start to pace. "We have to do something."

Carter grabs my shoulders, stopping my pacing. "That means you have to do something about *this*."

I look at the branches, tightly woven, keeping the inside room protected.

"High and mighty Mastermind revealed something in his little monologue," Carter says, a note of triumph in his voice. "Only Ophelia can let us in. I'm thinking these branches represent the walls she puts up around her heart. She's nearly impossible to get to know unless she lets you." Carter stares at me, willing me to understand. "So maybe it's not about just talking to her. Maybe this is about trying to *hear* her. And not just what you expect to hear. It's about what you *need* to hear."

He's right.

I hate when he's right.

But in this case, Ophelia's life is depending on me.

I touch the walls, closing my eyes. "Ophelia... can you hear me?"

44

Atlas

Eighteen Years Old

SURVIVING SCHOOL IS almost impossible without Moriah and Ophelia. I see Ophelia in the halls, but she's like a ghost. She moves through the crowds of students as if she is caught between reality and a different realm of existence.

I heard from some guys on the basketball team that Milo moved away. I can only assume that means he'd broken up with Ophelia, which is why she's a shell of a person as she roams the halls.

I don't try to reach out to her. She doesn't try to reach out to me.

I know I broke her trust in me at the funeral earlier this summer.

Any trust that was left, anyway.

Life is different now.

We aren't the kids we used to be, innocent children

with nothing more than dreams and stardust in our eyes.

We're growing up.

No one really talks about Moriah. The topic seems forbidden. Especially when I'm around. I've heard some whispers in the hallways, but whenever I come around, they quiet down.

I don't care; I won't see any of these people after graduation anyway.

I am numb to everything.

I'm also no fool. I don't think Moriah and I would've stayed together. But I do wish she were still alive.

I wish I hadn't turned Ophelia against me at the funeral. I wanted to pull her close, to comfort her. I wanted to hold her like old times. To act like the past few months had never happened.

Instead, I walked away from the only person who might've understood anything.

If the last few weeks have taught me anything, it's that this is how it was always meant to be.

I was meant to be alone.

45

OPHELIA IS CURLED up on the ground, the purple ball gown splayed around her. In the light, it shimmers with a haze of silver and gold.

"Atlas, please..." Ophelia whimpers.

His voice is clearly audible in the dome. But until he truly listens, he won't hear her.

"Ophelia, please say something," he calls.

I roll my eyes. How has she given him another chance?

Ophelia closes her eyes. "Atlas, I *am* saying something. You never hear me."

"I heard that. Barely. I'm sorry, Ophelia. I know you feel like I never truly hear you. I'm trying."

I straighten up on the ledge. If he's finally getting it, maybe this will get interesting.

She rises to her feet with difficulty. I hop off the ledge.

"Are you sure this is what you want?" I demand.

Ophelia turns back to look at me. "I don't want someone who would rather keep me in this gilded cage. Atlas is showing me what it is to open up again."

"I never said you'd stay in this cage. But I had to create it as part of your lesson, now, didn't I?"

She looks at me silently for a moment. "You didn't tell me much about how you ended up like this, Milo. How am I supposed to let you back in? I'm sorry we didn't work. I truly am. You're a wonderful person—"

I snort. "So wonderful I got stuck like this. Do you know how many souls I've eaten? Lives I've taken? Can you look me in the eyes and tell me I'm such a great human being?"

It's a bluff. I've never personally taken anyone's life. I've only eaten the souls and the auras provided by the other shadows. But I've still eaten. Still fed upon the innocent.

Ophelia steps close to me, her green eyes meeting my gray ones. Reya pulls at her hand, but Ophelia doesn't stop. "You are wracked with guilt and regret. You never wanted this to happen. You didn't want the darkness to consume you. And if you could go back, you'd change everything. I know you would. You're the guy who took me on the Ferris wheel at the summer carnival to help me forget about the boy who was breaking my heart. You're the guy who shared your funnel cake with me, even though you don't like to share your food. You're the one who let people expect the worse of you because you didn't care about what they thought. Milo, you're better than a lot of people. This curse... it doesn't define you."

Something shifts inside of me, coming undone. If I had the ability to cry, I probably would.

Ophelia steps back. "I'm only sorry that I can't be the one to break your curse."

"I thought it would be you," I say softly. "I really did."

"I can't be the one for you. I... I think I'm in love Atlas. And I'm not denying myself again. I'm sorry."

I nod my understanding, although I am filled with sorrow. "If you both figure out how to conquer this nightmare, you'll wake from your coma. But I will be stuck in this form. Halfway between shadow and human."

"Then maybe the one who can heal you is in the human world, not the Shadow Realm," she says gently.

I hold her gaze for a long moment. I hadn't considered that to be a possibility, that there could be someone for me other than Ophelia. Someone who could touch what is left of my heart and save me from this. Could someone like that really exist, someone who would even *want* to save me?

Ophelia studies me now, her heat tilted. "You use your shadows to conceal what you don't want the world to see."

I cross my arms. "So?"

"So why not try to expel them from yourself?"

I shake my head. "It doesn't work that way."

Ophelia nods, slowly. Her expression downcast, as though she wished she could change things for me. But it's too late. "Let someone else in," she says softly. "Let someone close enough to heal you."

I shake my head. "Someone like that does not exist

in this lifetime. No one is going to want to save me. Look at me, Ophelia. I'm a monster."

"You're not a monster. You're scared of what might happen if you let someone else love you. We were everything we needed in high school. You took care of me, and for that I thank you. I am forever thankful for you. But you have to let me go and let someone else carry the pieces of your heart that are broken. You may deny a heart exists beneath the shadows, but I can see it plainly."

I'm speechless, my mind reeling with possibility.

Ophelia walks to the wall and rests the palms of her hands against them. "Atlas, do you hear me?"

"Faintly."

"I want to trust you."

Wanting to trust someone and actually trusting someone are two different things. But I don't say that out loud. I can't. There are some aspects of the shadow magic that I cannot breach.

Atlas doesn't respond to Ophelia at first. Then he says, "So what can I do to make you feel safe? I know I've messed up in the past. But I regret everything I've ever done to hurt you. And I won't hurt you again."

Ophelia is silent for what feels like many bitter minutes. I know every moment of their past together is racing through her head. But she wants to let him in.

"I believe you," she says softly.

And then Atlas appears inside the dome.

46

Ophelia

"*A BROKEN HEART* isn't something that's easy to piece together."

Atlas kneels down to be next to me. His hands cup my face, his thumbs wiping away my tears.

His voice is soft. "I know. I've really screwed up. But I want to show you I can be different. I wasn't there for you when you needed me, even before Moriah died. And then I let her death become the excuse. There was never an excuse for leaving you behind."

I reach a hand up to hold one of his. "I want to let you in again, Atlas. Please make sure I don't regret it."

"I am going to piece together every part of your heart that I broke."

We rise together, and he pulls me to his chest. His heart beats against my cheek; his arms hold me protectively close.

In this moment, I feel safer than I ever have.

He presses a kiss to the top of my head, a gesture he's never done before.

Many old emotions flood back—fear, sadness, jealousy, loss—and I step away, looking over towards Milo. Atlas follows my gaze, then tenses.

"Milo? *You're* the Mastermind?"

Milo lazily leans against the wall. "Surprise. Did you miss me, Attie?"

Atlas's fists clench at his sides, but I grab one of his hands and gently open it, lacing my fingers with his. To Milo, I say, "We won, which means you won't eat our souls, right?"

To my horror, Milo smiles and shakes his head. "You haven't won yet, love. You'd be awake if your fear had been faced. But, yes, as soon as you figure out what you need to face in order to wake, you won't see me again in your nightmares. Unless someday my spell is broken and I can go where I please. I'd love to visit home."

Facing my fears means letting Atlas in. And to prove that I am really, truly willing to let my walls down, I know what I have to do.

"Atlas..."

He turns, his blue eyes taking me in. "Yeah?"

I lean up, my lips meeting his. Some part of me expects him to be shocked, to push me away. But his arms pull me closer. All around, I feel the walls crumbling. My senses are filled with Atlas. The taste of his lips and the feel of his hands pulling me closer and closer. The smell of his cologne and the forest around us.

My hands hold onto his shoulders as everything

else fades away. I don't think about the things that once stood between us.

We're here, in this moment.

And this moment is one I've dreamed of since I was fourteen. Maybe not quite this way, after so much hurt and so many broken hearts...

But as Atlas threads his fingers into my hair and the kiss becomes fiercer, stronger, full of longing and wishes, as we fall headlong into this moment between us, I finally allow myself to get lost in all the fairy tale endings I dreamed would happen.

And then I wake up.

47

Atlas

THE HOSPITAL ROOM is silent, save for the beeping of machines. I look around, though it's hard to see in the darkness.

Ophelia sighs. "Atlas?"

"I'm here," I say softly.

"Thank you for saving me."

"I'll always save you. I'm only sorry it took me so long."

We both fall silent for a moment, then I say, "I should probably get the nurses. They need to know you're awake. And I'm sure Reya will want to see you."

"You met Reya?"

"Something like that. She hasn't left the chair outside your room, no matter how many nurses ask her to go home."

Ophelia laughs, though it's soft. "You'll grow on her. Just give her time."

I rise from the chair and squeeze her hand before taking my hand gently from hers. I step out into the hall. There's a nurse standing a few feet away, writing something on a clipboard. She looks up at me. "She's awake."

The nurse's eyes widen and she rushes past me into the room, turning on the lights.

Reya's asleep in the chair, her head tilted back slightly to rest against the wall behind her. I consider for a moment waking her up, but she appears to be out cold. I follow the nurse back into the room.

Ophelia squints at first as her eyes adjust to the brightness.

The nurse begins asking her a ton of questions and checking different vitals. I stand against the wall, letting the nurse do her job.

The nurse sighs as she finishes up. "I'm so glad you woke up. We were truly worried about you. We'll have to do another head scan in the morning. Until then, rest."

"I feel like staying up," Ophelia says.

"I'm sure you're pretty wide awake now. We were able to contact your father, and he's on his way. Your phone wasn't badly damaged, so we were able to find your emergency contacts. It took a while to get ahold of him, but he should be here as soon as possible. He said he works far away from here."

Ophelia nods. But there's relief in her eyes knowing her dad is coming.

He's always buried himself in his work after his wife, Ophelia's mom, left them. Even though he's gone a lot, he's here when it counts. He cares so much for Ophelia. I imagine he's beside himself right now.

The nurse raises the head of Ophelia's bed so she can sit up a bit, then leaves to inform the doctor. Ophelia looks over to her bedside table and then back at me. "Can you hand me my phone?"

"Yeah."

I walk to where it sits. The screen is cracked, but it works otherwise. "When you get out of here, I can take you to the store in the city to get a new one," I offer.

Ophelia smiles sadly. "Thanks. I'm sure I won't have a car for a while."

"Consider me your personal chauffeur." I give a mock bow and a gentle smile.

"Thankfully, I can walk to work when I want. I should call Priya first."

"Would you like me to step outside? Give you privacy?"

"No. Please stay."

She scoots over on the bed, patting the space where no wires are. I slide on and edge up next to her. She makes her phone calls with her free hand, and I gently hold onto her other hand, which is still tethered by tubes and wires.

She calls Priya first. Priya is absolutely beside herself when Ophelia tells her about the accident. I can tell by the way Ophelia tries her best to comfort her.

Then Ophelia calls her father.

He answers after the first ring, and Ophelia starts to cry at the sound of his voice. I hold her tighter, doing my best to comfort her. From what I can tell, her father says he's about an hour away, but he's going to be here as soon as he can.

After she finishes with her phone calls, I set the phone on the bedside table for her.

"I'm glad you're the one they called," she whispers. "I don't think I'd want anyone else here. Don't tell Reya I said that, though."

"Trust me, she cares for you more than you know. She interrogated me before I came in the room," I quip. Then my voice grows serious. "But I'm glad you want me here. I don't deserve it after abandoning you when you needed me. Even before Moriah died. I'm so sorry I wasn't here for you." It feels like I can never, ever say that enough.

Ophelia settles closer to me. "I don't regret being with Milo. But I feel sorry for... how he ended up. I hope he'll come out of this."

"I wouldn't want you to regret Milo," I tell her truthfully. He was a friend to her when I wasn't.

My phone rings abruptly. I turn to pull it out of my pocket with my free hand. Carter's picture flashes on the screen. I put it to my ear. "Hello?"

"Yes, I made it back out of the nightmare alive. Thank you for asking."

"I'm sorry. I was distracted."

"You disappeared into the dome and then next thing I know I was awake."

I cringe. "You have every right to be mad. Ophelia just woke up from the coma, and it's just been one thing after another since we were all in that dome. I'm sorry, bro."

"You're forgiven, but only for Ophelia's sake. I'm really glad she's okay. I'll come see her in the morning."

After a quick goodbye, I hang up. Ophelia drifts off to sleep beside me, and soon I join her, finally in a dreamless sleep.

48

Rook

WATCHING OPHELIA AND Atlas lie side by side breaks my heart. I'm grateful that I'm still invisible to those who are awake. I wanted to check on Ophelia one last time.

Atlas lies beside her, his fingers intertwined with hers. They sleep, but they don't dream. At least, not dreams that I can access.

When I step out of the hospital room, there's a girl sitting in a chair outside the door. A nurse is begging her to leave.

The girl's arms are crossed, her hair a bright pink that's begun to fade into a softer pink at the roots.

The nurse looks rather annoyed. "Miss Reya, I understand this is hard, but visiting hours are in the morning. You will be welcome to come back then and visit your friend. But right now, she needs her rest."

Reya. I remember her from high school. She

became Ophelia's friend right after Ophelia and I broke up.

The nurse sighs. "Look, I don't want to have to call security. Please, sweetheart. Go home, rest, and come back in the morning."

"Why does Atlas get to stay at all hours, but I can't see my best friend for a few minutes before I go home?"

"Because he was the point of contact that answered first. Until her father gets here, we are allowing him to stay so she doesn't feel alone.

The nurse glances around the hallway, then lowers her voice. "If you come at seven, I'll let you see her, even though visiting hours start at nine. You have to be here in this chair right at seven, though. Because my shift ends soon after."

Reya finally stands. "All right, fine. I'll do it your way this time."

She stalks off down the hallway, and I follow her. I admire her ferocious spirit, and I have a need to consume the wildness of her dreams. I crave her energy, her strength.

Maybe Ophelia was right.

Maybe it's time I look for the cure in other places.

EPILOGUE
Ophelia

A FEW WEEKS have passed since the accident. I'm home, though not alone very often. My father was beside himself that he wasn't here for me. He quit his jobs, and he's decided to search for one that will allow him to be with me more.

I don't know how I feel about it quite yet, as he hovers over me constantly, despite my constant reassurances that I'm okay.

I've returned to work, too. Some days I walk there. When Atlas is in town visiting his mom, he drives me. Priya doesn't let me work too hard, though.

"You know, at this rate, you're wasting money on me," I say, "if you won't let me do my job."

"You are doing your job. I'll tell you when you aren't," Priya says, smiling as she scolds me. "Now I want you to stay sitting behind the counter. And drink your water."

I roll my eyes and smirk, but I can feel the warmth behind her words.

The bell above the door rings as Atlas comes in. Priya smiles brightly at him, but waggles her eyebrows at me. A light blush spreads across my cheeks as he comes over and kisses my forehead.

"How's the love of my life?"

"Aww," Priya coos. "You two are so cute together. I'm so glad everything worked out for you in the end."

Atlas smiles at her, then turns his attention back to me. "I am, too. Now, how are you doing? I mean it."

"I'd be fine if everyone didn't treat me like a fragile flower who's going to fall apart at any moment."

"Bah," Priya mutters. "I'm sorry I'm concerned about my favorite person in this town."

"Yeah, yeah, all right. Just chill out a little and let me do a little more work."

"Next week, I'll consider it. For now, you sit there and look pretty. Doesn't she look pretty, Atlas?"

Atlas looks me up and down, though I doubt a pullover hoodie and leggings gives him much to look at. "The most beautiful woman *I've* seen."

I roll my eyes. "All right, what do you want?"

"Can't I compliment my girlfriend for no reason?"

"You often do. But there's an undertone in your words."

"I want to take you and your father to dinner."

Priya chokes on a sip of water, her eyes full of shock and laughter. As she sputters and coughs in the corner, she gives me a thumbs up. I shake my head at her before returning my gaze to Atlas. "Okay. I'll text him."

"No need. I already stopped by your house and asked him. He's in my truck. We just wanted to come get you."

I look over at Priya, but she beats me to it. "Yes, she will go to dinner. Her shift is just about over. Go get food," she says, having recovered from her coughing attack.

"I see you and my father are playing me," I say teasingly, narrowing my eyes at Atlas.

"Me? Never. I just wanted to sweeten the deal for when I ask if you can come stay with me in the city for the weekend. I want to assure him there's no funny business."

"But funny business is my favorite business," I tease.

Atlas blushes, a rare sight. I always feel victorious when I'm the cause of it. "You know what I meant."

"Yes, I did. Don't worry. My dad adores you. But thank you for coming to ask him so I didn't have to. I *am* an adult who can make my own decisions, though."

"I know. It's about showing respect. But I will not be mentioning that we'll have to share a bed."

"I could mention we have before."

Atlas blushes again.

Priya grins and shakes her head at the two of us.

We walk to his truck in the small parking lot behind the bookstore. My dad lounges in the backseat, leaning forward eagerly when Atlas opens my door and helps me in.

"I'm very excited about this dinner," he says.

"Hello to you, too."

"Sorry. I'm hungry. I was thrilled when Atlas came by and asked to take us to dinner."

My heart swells. I want to capture moments like

these in a photo or a poem and keep them forever, tucked away somewhere that I can look back on someday.

The look of pride on my dad's face. The feel of Atlas's hand in mine as he drives us to the diner. The way my dad and Atlas talk so easily, as if no time has passed. The way Atlas looks at me as though I'm the most beautiful work of art he's ever seen.

I do worry about Milo sometimes. Some nights, before I fall asleep, I try to open my mind up, in case he wants to visit. But he never does.

I know I made the right choice. Milo and I were a wild moment. A candle burning bright, but not everlasting. I cherish the moments we shared, and I will forever regard them as some of my most treasured ones.

But I couldn't keep him. He belongs to someone else who can love him and break the curse.

I let my mind drift away from those darker thoughts of worry, letting it sink back into the present.

Into dinner with my boyfriend and my dad.

Into the drive home as the sun dips behind the clouds.

Into the moment my dad goes inside to give Atlas and me a few minutes alone before he starts his long drive to the city.

"So, I'll come by after work Friday and pick you up. We can go to dinner and then maybe catch a movie."

"That sounds perfect."

I rest my head on his shoulder as we stare up into the sky. As the stars begin to shine, Atlas's lips find mine.

And finally, everything is as it should be.

ACKNOWLEDGEMENTS

At the end of every book, I sit here thinking up all the things I want to say to the people that made this possible. I get emotional writing these because there are so many people who have taken the time to support me on this journey of chasing my dreams.

First, I start by thanking God. Thank you for giving me this passion to write books and do something with my words. God, you have gifted me with this passion and I know You will see me through to chase my dreams.

To my parents, for always supporting me in chasing my dreams. Thank you for instilling in me the perseverance to never give up.

To my siblings, who are probably my biggest cheerleaders. I appreciate knowing you read my books.

To Faith, for always reading what I write. Thank you for being a very honest and wise critique partner and for editing this book when I felt lost. You saved my heart from breaking further when I thought this book was hopeless. More than that, thank you for being my friend.

To Bree, my fellow INFP fangirl. You have cheered on this book to anyone and everyone who will listen and I cannot thank you enough for that. Thank you for reading it before it was edited. I know it was a bit of a mess, but you fell in love with it anyway. Thank you. And thank you for your friendship.

To the discord writing fam, you guys have been some of the loudest and biggest supporters I've had. But not only that, you've been good friends. I can't wait to see what the future holds for your writing endeavors. I would name each and every one of you, and why you are amazing and what you've done for me, but then I'd have a whole other book. But you know who each of you are and I appreciate you all.

To Jen, my editor, for guiding me when I felt so lost about this book. Your edits have always made me feel seen and understood. I don't think there is an editor out there who can rival your skill. I hope every writer finds an editor like you!

To Stefanie, my cover designer, thank you for making me so happy with the cover. And for being so patient while you waited for the final details to finish the wrap. You rock!

To Abbie Emmons, who has been one of the reasons I even began this journey. I don't think I would be this far in my author career if you hadn't helped me with every step. Thank you for answering every question I have and for always being willing to help me out. Formatting books would be a nightmare without your knowledge. But more important than the books and the writing, thank you for being my friend!

And to you, dear reader. This book was hard to write. I didn't think I would ever be able to complete another book once Raegan and Peter's story was over. This book showed me that I can still write something without living with the characters for seven years. It was a challenge, but I'm so glad it exists now.

Thank you for taking a chance on this book, wherever it may have found you. I hope it touches the broken parts of your heart and soothes the ache in your bones.

With Love,

Brooke Riley

ABOUT THE AUTHOR

 BROOKE RILEY found her love of writing in High School. Her love of words developed much earlier in her life. She was reading books as soon as she learned how, and her love of literature never stopped. When she isn't writing, she's most likely making Spotify playlists for future writing projects, or putting together Pinterest boards for said writing projects. She can also be found reading or playing Fortnite in her free time.

CONNECT WITH BROOKE RILEY

INSTAGRAM: @thebrookeriley

TIKTOK: @thebrookeriley